Praise for *The Lifeguard*

"The stories are quite disarmingly complex, while keeping up a surface appearance of clarity and straightforwardness.... It's a fine book."

—Charles Baxter

"Ten subtle, impressionistic stories that linger and expand in the memory."

—*Mademoiselle*

"Mary Morris's compassion is on par with her sense of humor, a rare combination...."

—Betsy Willeford, *Star-Ledger*
(Newark, New Jersey)

"As a storyteller, Morris shines. Reading her best stories is like sinking into a good photograph. She packs them with tiny details, but never allows the particulars to interfere with the vision and balance of the whole."

—Julia Corbin, *St. Petersburg Times*

"[A] poised and articulate collection."

—*Publishers Weekly*

"Exquisitely revealing moments...clearly Morris hasn't lost her touch as a story writer."

—*Kirkus Reviews*

"Morris's ability to reincarnate her travel stories into fiction make for a well-rounded, fully formed body of work. It is also a pleasure to come upon a contemporary author who writes fiction and nonfiction equally well."

—Kristin Rose, *Ft. Lauderdale Sun-Sentinel*

"What really unifies these stories is Morris's spartan approach to descriptive detail and her spare language. Instead of spoon-feeding her readers, Morris leaves much for them to infer."

—Marie Elsie St. Léger, *Time Out New York*

BY MARY MORRIS

THE
Lifeguard

MARY MORRIS

PICADOR USA
NEW YORK

Picador® USA is a registered trademark and is used by St. Martin's Press under license from Pan Books Limited.

For information on Picador USA Reading Group Guides, as well as ordering, please contact the Trade Marketing department at St. Martin's Press.
Phone: 1-800-221-7945 extension 488
Fax: 212-677-7456
E-mail: trademarketing@stmartins.com

Some of the stories in this collection have appeared, in slightly different form, in the following publications: "The Lifeguard" and "Losing Track" in the *Boston Globe;* "The Lure" in *The Breadloaf Anthology of Contemporary American Short Stories;* "Slice of Life" in *Listening to Ourselves;* "The Wall" in *Vogue;* "Souvenirs" in *Epoch;* "Around the World" in *Crosscurrents* and *Best of the West;* "The Moon Garden" in *McCall's* (as "A Season for Growth"; "The Glass-Bottom Boat" in the *Midwesterner.*

With special thanks to Sloan Harris and Jessica Green at ICM who helped these stories find homes.

ISBN 0-312-18694-0

First published in the United States by Nan A. Talese, an imprint of Doubleday, a division of the Bantam Doubleday Dell Publishing Group, Inc.

First Picador USA Paperback Edition: June 1998

10 9 8 7 6 5 4 3 2 1

*This book of stories is dedicated to the
memory of Peter St. John, in whose house
many of them were written.*

Contents

THE
Lifeguard

THE Lifeguard

The summer before I left for college, I was head lifeguard on the beach at Pirate's Point. I don't think real pirates ever landed there, but the name made me think that strange and mysterious things could happen right where I lived. I grew up on that peninsula, and it was my home. I never found it monotonous, staring across the sea, but instead I liked to think of what lay beyond, how someday perhaps I'd sail to the other side.

The beach was a long strip of what had once been white sand but was now beginning to turn darker and less pristine. It was lined with striped umbrellas and beach chairs. I loved the gentle easing of the beach umbrellas into the sand, the smell of Coppertone on my skin, the way people looked up when I blew my whistle, their faces always with a slight look of terror that one of theirs had been swept up, ever since the drowning of Billy Mandel.

For four years of my youth I was the lifeguard there. I'd watched this beach, where I'd spent my summers as a boy, red bucket and shovel in hand, fill with more and more umbrellas. I had watched the boys who were lifeguards turn flabby. I had seen Ric Spencer, who had ruled this beach before me for half a decade, lose his hair, and I'd seen the slim bodies of women stretch with childbearing. I'd seen it all and it had not impressed me, but rather it flowed through me like a river, not stopping here.

I was eighteen then. I wore zinc oxide on my nose, a whistle around my neck. No. 4 Coppertone covered my body. I could lift a girl into the air with each arm, and I loved to walk the beach, a girl dangling from each bicep. Girls clung to my stand, like the shipwrecked to their raft, and I could do no wrong.

It would have been a perfect summer for me, were it not for Mrs. Lovenheim. Every day at the same time, about ten in the morning, Mrs. Lovenheim came. She never had to ask me to set up her red-and-white umbrella because she always came at the same time each day, so I was ready for her. Mrs. Lovenheim stretched out like a cat, opened a book, which she held open at almost the same page every day, and stayed like that for hours, then went away. She never went near the water or sat in the sun. She never walked to the hot-dog stand but instead just stayed beneath her umbrella, straw hat on her head. That was all she did, except it seemed as though Mrs. Lovenheim never took her eyes off of me.

She was perhaps only thirty then but seemed very old. She had flaming red hair and a small, compact body. She'd been married to a real estate broker who'd dropped her, my mother told me, after she'd miscarried two babies. She could not hold them, my mother whispered to me one evening in a darkened corner of the den where my own father had drunk beer and watched TV sports, until he died suddenly during a winter storm, and this secret world of women seemed ever closed to me.

I did not care for such things—for women who could and could not hold babies, for women who had been left in the middle of their lives, alone. I had girls who loved me—the girls of summer, with their bronzed skin and naked unblemished bellies, and it would have been a perfect summer for me, this last summer of my youth, if I had not felt that at each moment my every move was being watched by Mrs. Lovenheim, who never spoke unless she wanted something or rose until it was time to go home. If I had not felt that while my eyes were on the water Mrs. Lovenheim's were on me.

Ric Spencer came on weekends with his wife, Sally, and their daughter, Becky. Sally used to babysit for me when I was a boy, and she'd make big vats of hot chocolate, which we'd sip in front of late movies. She liked the really scary

movies in which giant pods swallowed people or where something came out of the muck, terrorizing a neighborhood, and
Sally clutched my hand whenever the frightening thing appeared, making me feel, even though she was taking care of me,
as if I were the one who was taking care of her.

Then she married Ric Spencer, and some say she had to.
Becky was born not long after their marriage, and Sally's days
in bikinis were done. On weekdays Sally and her mother, Mrs.
Winston, who used to be our neighbor, came alone to the
beach. But on the weekend Ric came as well, and I could see
him, lying listlessly on the sand, bored within the confines of his
family. And when he could get away from them, he'd plant
himself beneath my stand.

He'd been on duty when the Mandel boy disappeared, and it
was a story he liked to tell. The drowning of Billy Mandel was
the only recorded drowning in the history of Pirate's Point, and
the first time Ric told me about the Mandel boy it was like a
warning to me, not that the drowning had been Ric's fault. But
then over many Saturdays beneath my stand, the story grew and
improved. "It was like this," Ric said, beads of sweat shimmering on the place where his hair used to be. In his glory Ric had
had a taut swimmer's body and thick blond curls. "It was this
quick thing." A split second when a child is playing with a
bucket by the shore and the father looks up, distracted, by the
call of a friend. Ric would make up dialogue for me. "Hey,
Joe, how'ya doing? How about dinner with us next Saturday?"
Or, "I see the wife's got you working."

Innocuous words like that, and when the father looked back,

when he let his gaze turn to the place where the sea met the shore, where Billy had been digging just moments before, there was a blank space, a void where he'd been taken by a wave, not a very big wave, but big enough to pull him under. While my own eyes scanned the water, Ric loved to describe the search of the beach, the lifeguards' patrol. He'd describe himself, swimming endlessly along the shoreline, until the sea brought Billy Mandel back hours later, bloated and having strangely taken on the color of the sea.

That summer the girls would not stay away, and I'd have to hold them at bay. They'd offer to buy me things—Cokes, hot dogs—and rub cream on my back while I sat like an idol perched in my chair. I liked being above them because I could see down the front of their bathing suits, and even though they knew I was looking at their breasts, they did nothing to hide.

There was Cindy Hartwick, with her thick black hair, whom I dated sometimes on Saturday nights when my mom gave me the car. And Sara Clarkson, who would be beautiful as soon as her braces came off. And there was Peggy Mandel. Sometimes I'd look across the beach and see Mr. and Mrs. Mandel with their daughter, a girl almost my age now, their only child. Peggy, who was a sophomore and known to be fast, used to shout at her parents, who sat motionless, reading endless newspapers unless Peggy went for a swim. And then Mr. Mandel would stand in his sneakers, waves lapping at his feet, as if somehow, through his attentiveness, he could bring back what was gone.

I was above them all from my stand, where my eyes scanned the beach like a beacon. I could see the Spencers under their blue-and-yellow umbrella and watch Becky go toddling away. When Ric was there, Becky went naked and got to eat sand, but when it was just the women, Becky stayed dressed. And there was Mr. Potter, who'd had a heart attack and walked with small weights in his hands, up and down the shoreline. And there was Mrs. Lovenheim, always there watching my every move whenever the girls came around.

My dreams at night were like the dreams of other boys—I dreamed of the bodies of girls, dreams that woke me from my sleep, leaving me sweaty, the sheets twisted around me. Dreams that made me rise in the middle of the night and throw the window open, until my mother, who never slept well in the big bed after my father died, shouted, "Are you all right? Is anything wrong?" Those were most of my dreams, but there were others, dreams of water, and sometimes there was a nightmare that came to me. In it I see myself from a perspective that is high. I am a boy with a bucket in my hand playing in the setting of parents, umbrellas, buckets, and shovels. And then from behind me, always behind me, as I dig a hole in the sand, the sea is rising, black and surging against the sky.

All summer long, when he could sneak away, Ric Spencer came and sat at the base of my lifeguard stand and talked about the old days. Ric had been my teacher for Red Cross training and taught me what I know about riptides and undertows and sudden changes on the surface of the sea. He was only twenty-six that summer when I became head lifeguard, but he used to say, as bronzed girls handed me Cokes or asked if I needed more oil on my back, "Man, you don't know what it is. You don't know what you've got." He'd always say it in the same way, so finally one day I said to him, "What is it, Ric? What've I got?"

He extended his arms as if to encompass the beach. "You've got all this. It's yours."

I laughed, not understanding what he meant. "You know," he went on, "I've got this job, I sell computer parts. I go to these retail stores all over New England, even in the winter, when it's freezing cold, and I think to myself how I wish I were anywhere else doing anything else, but what can I do?"

He pointed over to Mrs. Lovenheim, who was looking our way, her novel lying flat on her blanket. "You know, I knew her when. Before she married that guy who dumped her." I looked over at Mrs. Lovenheim, and she did not look away. I couldn't imagine that anyone could have known her "when," whenever that was. "She was something," Ric said. He whistled between his teeth.

Just then Cindy Hartwick appeared, with a hot dog for me with everything on it, one I hadn't even asked for, and she handed it up. Then Peggy Mandel strutted by in a bikini, to her father's dismay. I tipped my visor, then Ric went on. "You don't know," he said, "how lucky you are."

loved my body that summer. I loved its firmness and its
bronzed skin. But mostly I loved the way it was admired.
Girls I didn't know would come up and squeeze parts of me.
Old people looked at me, their bodies covered with chicken
skin and blue veins, as if I were an object in the museum that
had become their lives. So I loved to stroll the beach among the
girls who wanted to have me, old men who wanted to be me.

Sitting in my chair was harder, because the thing about being
a lifeguard is that your eyes should be set on the sea. You watch
for nothing, really, and sometimes you begin to see things. I've
seen what I thought were the tidal waves of my dreams, heading
straight for me, but it was only the meeting of a cloud and the
sea. I've seen monsters rise from the belly of the deep when it's
only a big fish leaping into the air. And then I've seen things
that aren't there at all. I've seen people before my eyes disappear. And sometimes I've even heard cries for help from behind
the waves. But these are all lifeguard mirages, and they happen
to anyone who looks at one thing too long.

But at times it was hard for me to keep looking out, and so I
welcomed the company of girls. Though I'd never intended to
do this, one day I asked out Peggy Mandel. She had come to
hand me a Coke, and I'd gazed down at her. Then I said, quite
simply, "Would you like to go to a movie Saturday night?"

On Saturday night I picked up Peggy. She wore a pink cotton
dress with spaghetti straps, and her parents stood at the door,
despondent, as if I were taking her to live in another country,
saying useless things like "Come back soon." I watched them

curiously, these people whose life had been irrevocably altered with the sweep of a wave.

We went to a drive-in, where I let my arm dangle against the seat. She leaned her head into my arm, and I felt her breath against my chest. I pulled her closer to me, and she raised her head toward mine, bringing her lips to my lips. She was warm and alive, and I knew I could have almost anything I wanted with her. I leaned my own face close to hers. "Tell me about Billy," I heard myself say.

She pulled away slightly at first. "What?" she said. She was flushed and drowsy, like someone who has been asleep.

"About Billy. I want to know."

She sat back, tossing her dark brown hair. "Billy?"

"Your brother, the one who drowned," as if she didn't know. "Tell me about it."

Her face looked the way I've seen girls look, amazed and sickened, in biology labs when a rodent is about to be splayed. "You want to know about Billy? Why do you want to know about Billy? Why do you want to know about Billy?"

"I don't know. Tell me what happened." I couldn't explain why, but I wanted to know what it is like when you look at a patch of sand and a part of your life is gone. What does she imagine it felt like to be deep in the sea? Maybe it was because Ric Spencer had talked about it so much, but I wanted her to tell me what no one else could.

"What happened? You want to know what happened?"

I realized she thought my request was odd. "I'm the lifeguard," I said. "I don't want to make any mistakes."

9

"Okay, I'll tell you what happened." She was furious now and looked old for her years. "My dad looked away, and Billy drowned, and nobody's ever been the same. Is that what you want to know?"

"I want to know what he was like. Did you play with him when he was small?"

"I was four years old and my brother drowned." She flung her body to the opposite side of the car so that the door made a jangling sound, as if someone were trying to get in. "You're sick," she said under her breath. "Now take me home."

The day it happened was a day of particular calm. A Saturday when a gentle southwest wind blew. A day when the waves hardly lapped and it was almost hypnotic for me to keep my eyes fixed on the sea. It is easier to look at roughness and fast-breaking waves, and that day I was having trouble staying awake.

Ric Spencer stood beneath my lifeguard stand that morning. He stood there and said, "You know what, man, I've been thinking. I could do something else with my life. I mean, I could go to night school. Maybe become a coach. I don't have to do this door-to-door crap."

"Hey," I told him, "there's plenty you could do."

"That's just what I've been thinking. I've been thinking about opening a little retail store, maybe software. What d'ya think?" He seemed happy just having said this when Cindy

Hartwick came by with a Coke; Ric winked and drifted away. "Catch you later," he said, heading back to his umbrella.

"Hey," Cindy said. "What're you doing after work?" I gazed down for a moment. Cindy wore a turquoise two-piece, and she had straight black hair and black eyes. She began climbing up my stand like a monkey, laughing, "Hey, so what are you doing?"

Then Peggy Mandel walked by. "He's a sicko," she shouted. "He's weird."

"Not as weird as you, Mandel," I called back. "Not like you."

"Oh, yeah? Go to a drive-in with him. You'll see."

"What's she talking about?" Cindy asked.

"Oh, it's nothing," I said. But Peggy had disturbed me. Now Cindy was reaching up, and I thought I'd take her out on Saturday night. I didn't have to look; I could feel Mrs. Lovenheim's eyes on me. Cindy kept reaching for me, and, as if I thought it would drive Mrs. Lovenheim wild, I pretended to pull Cindy up to my stand.

It was perhaps only an instant that I was distracted, but suddenly I was aware of the shouting, and it took me by surprise. At first I thought I was hearing things, but it was too loud and clear. Perhaps I'd had my eyes off the sea for one minute, maybe two. No more than that. Perhaps for the first time all summer I'd completely forgotten where I was. Now my instincts took over. I let go of Cindy and stood up straight in my chair. Grabbing my binoculars, I scanned the water for signs—

the flailing arms, a bobbing head, the gathering of crowds, parents diving—but there was nothing, nothing at all. But still I heard the shouting, so I leaped to the sand and began to race up and down the shore.

That was when I saw Ric Spencer, running across the burning sand, waving his hands in an awkward way. He ran forward, then back, then forward again, like a dog wanting to play catch. He kept waving, shouting, then rushing back again. Then Mr. Potter, whose own failing heart kept him pacing the shore, came puffing to me. "A child," he said with surprising composure. "Over there," pointing to the Spencer umbrella.

I was amazed by this, taken off guard. While I had been searching ahead, what had happened was behind me. A crowd had gathered around the blue and yellow umbrella. The Mandels put their newspaper down and started walking, Mrs. Mandel clinging to her husband's arm. I saw a small frenzy of people moving up and down. I ran toward Ric. He caught me in his arms. "It's Becky." He shook me like a wet towel. "Get your kit. Get your damn kit."

I dashed back to my stand, grabbed the first-aid kit, and raced, my own feet searing on the sand. I made my way through where the crowd had gathered and saw Becky Spencer, her face puffed, her mouth open but no sound coming, her eyes in a fixed stare, turning as blue as the sea I'd set my sights on, and I knew this was the color of Billy Mandel when he'd been tossed back to the shore.

"She swallowed something," Ric said. He shook violently.

"Do something, man." Tears fell down his cheeks. "I've tried everything. God, please do something."

"You've killed her," Mrs. Winston, on her knees, shouted. "You've killed your daughter." And Sally, tears streaming down her face, kept banging her daughter on the back.

"Turn her over," I said, and I tipped Becky upside down, pounding on her back, but no breath came from her, no sound. I tipped her again, like an hourglass, but still nothing came. Then I clutched the dying child in my arms.

"You've killed her," Mrs. Winston shrieked, pointing at Ric. "You'll live with this forever."

Sally Spencer, who'd once dug her nails into my arm during the horror movies of my youth, now did so again. "You're the lifeguard," she said matter-of-factly. "You're supposed to know what to do." But I'd done everything I'd been trained to do, and nothing could bring Becky Spencer, her mouth gaping in a silent, breathless hole, back to life.

It was then that I saw Mrs. Lovenheim close her book, take off her hat, and rise. I saw that woman, left and bereft, who had languished all summer beneath her umbrella, coming toward us, her red hair wild in the breeze, and like Moses she parted the spectators, the advisers, the lookers-on. She pushed the screaming mother away, shoved the accusatory grandmother onto the hot sand. She thrust Ric into the background and plucked the dying child from my arms, forcing me to my knees.

She held Becky, the child's face the shade of the deepest re-
cesses of the sea, her body rigid and motionless. Then Mrs.
Lovenheim wrapped her body around Becky's, folded the blue
breathless body into her own.

I watched from my knees as the woman whose beach umbrella I had planted day after day, whose chairs I had arranged,
who had tipped me poorly, whose face was beset by the grief of
her own failed marriage, who nursed what I now recognize to
be a broken heart, Mrs. Lovenheim, perhaps not more than
thirty then, grappled the child into her arms, engulfed her as if
bringing her back into her own womb, then pressed some place
I had not found. She squeezed Becky above the navel three
times with a force I'd never before seen in nature, until a
perfect, unblemished green grape shot like a bullet from the
child's mouth.

Becky gasped and spit as Mrs. Lovenheim handed the whim-
pering child to her mother, who sobbed in the sand. For the
first time the grandmother was silent. Ric stood shaking, his life
altered. Then Mrs. Lovenheim turned to me where I stood,
first-aid kit dangling in my hand like a lunch box. I felt as if she
were about to say or do something, but instead, without a
word, she moved past me back to her umbrella, collected her
things, and left.

That night I could not sleep. It was late, and I wasn't sure
what was bothering me, so I went downstairs. I sat in my
father's chair in the darkened den until I knew what I wanted to

do. I found the address in the phone book. Then I got into the car and drove. I drove along the ocean road until I was a block short of her house, and I parked there.

It was a clear night at the end of August, and a salt breeze blew off the ocean. It was a nice night for a walk along the shore, so I took my time, sucking in my breath. Then I headed down the street until I reached the house where she lived. The lights were on upstairs, but I stood for a long time on the porch. Then I knocked on the door, softly at first, then louder.

At last she descended the stairs. She wore a yellow robe, tied around her waist, and her red hair fell to her shoulders. "Yes?" Mrs. Lovenheim said, her voice warm like a breeze.

"It's me," I said, "Josh Michaels."

She slowly opened the door, only partially at first. She looked at me oddly, as if trying to remember when she'd seen me before. "I'm the lifeguard," I said, not knowing what else to say. And it suddenly occurred to me that she had no idea who I was, that she'd never really seen me at all. So I added foolishly, "At the beach."

"Yes," she mumbled. "What is it?"

"I wanted to thank you," I said, not really knowing why I'd come. "I wanted to thank you for what you did. This afternoon."

She cocked her head. "Oh, it's just something I learned. I take silly courses sometimes."

"But I didn't know what to do," I mumbled. I was not aware as I said it that tears streamed down my face. But soon I found myself crying on Mrs. Lovenheim's porch, on the porch of the woman to whom I was, in fact, nothing at all. I dropped my shoulders and stood there, sobbing. ''I didn't know what to do.''

I don't know how long I stood there like that before she reached for me, pulled me to her, wrapped her arms around mine. She smelled of shampoo and oils, not the salt and sand I'd expected. It was the first time I felt what it was supposed to feel like to be in the arms of a woman, not the girls whose breath steamed my car on Saturday nights. But it was not her body I felt, though I liked the feel of it, it was not her sex, though I was aware of it. Rather, I felt myself longing for something I could never have, and I wanted her to take me back, fold me inside of herself as she'd folded Becky that afternoon.

But then she let me go. I grabbed at her, trying to hold on, as if her arms could save me from what came next. But without a word she went inside. ''Wait,'' I said, ''come back.'' I knew I would never want anyone or anything as much as I wanted Mrs. Lovenheim right then, and I found myself slipping into despair as she released me back into the world.

It was the last time I saw Mrs. Lovenheim that summer, or any other summer, for that matter. Or perhaps I saw her again, but we no longer recognized each other. It was my last summer on the beach, and after that the winds shifted, the weather changed, which would bring my departure for college. Years have passed since that day on Pirate's Point, and I am old now, perhaps as old as Mrs. Lovenheim was then, and I've never seen the water or the umbrellas of summer in the same way again.

THE Wall

When Meg moved in with Zachary, he said she could do anything she wanted to fix the place up, except paint the wall. She liked the house well enough. It was colonial-style, white with green shutters, and most of what she didn't like Zachary said she could throw out. There was the accumulated junk—the old roller skates in the basement from children who wouldn't be caught dead in them now, the three-legged Ping-Pong table, newspapers from terror-stricken Sundays, the foreign coins from too many business trips, napkins stained with the assorted sauces Lucinda made that never came out right and never turned things around.

Meg scrutinized this house of dead plants that drooped like eavesdroppers in the living room, and dreary cacti that would never bloom, of burnt-down candles and cat-clawed sofas, the paint-chipped ceilings that fell on Meg like the sky on Chicken Little, and the closets filled with Lucinda's clothing—the clothing of a flower child of the sixties. All this debris, Zachary said, she could do away with. "You can do whatever you want," he told her as they carried in her boxes. "You just can't paint the wall."

The wall, which was in the kitchen, was quite large and was covered with a mural. It had an angel rising out of a cloud, grasping a lightning bolt, standing in the Urubamba Valley amidst Aztec burial mounds, the pyramids of Egypt, and the oracle at Delphi, in the shadow of the Taj Mahal, encircled by the Great Wall, protected by a moat where snakes and lizards swam, beyond which rabbits, birds, buffalo, and squirrels scattered as if before a brushfire across a field of giant sunflowers that covered the ceiling.

The first time Meg saw the wall was the morning after she'd first stayed with Zachary. She hadn't seen it the night before when he'd brought her home in the dark, snuck her upstairs, and wildly pulled every piece of clothing off her before carrying her to the king-size former marital bed that hadn't been used in this capacity, he told her in the midst of his passion, in almost a decade. It was a rare weekend when Lucinda had the kids, and Meg had tiptoed down in the morning to make coffee, feeling relaxed, her body at peace. When Zachary came down a few minutes later, he found her staring, not knowing what to say. Finally she was able to speak. "Why sunflowers?" she asked.

"Because Lucinda liked sunflowers," Zachary replied.

Meg loved all the rooms of the house, except the kitchen. She loved their old-fashioned feel. She could deal with the modern built-ins in the colonial house, the palé oak against the walnut floors. She could live with the mysterious fact that all the furniture was nailed down—that beds and tables and sofas could not be moved. Or with the fact that the bed was so big she woke up sometimes feeling confused about where she was, the way she did in foreign countries.

What she could not deal with was the wall. It had been painted by a friend of Lucinda's, an artist named Mona. Mona had felt a profound connection to Lucinda and Zachary, to their children, and she had painted this mural, Zachary told Meg, as guardian and safekeeper of home. She wanted to depict the enduring spirit of man in the face of the rise and fall of civilization. Zachary admitted it wasn't the best thing Mona had ever done, but "as long as we live in this house, until we get a place of our own, we'll just have to live with it."

"Out of loyalty to whom?" Meg had asked, concerned that somehow he could not move on to the next phase of his life.

"To Mona," Zachary had replied. "To a friend."

Examining the closet where some of Lucinda's rejects still hung, Meg said, "I'm not sure I can sleep in another woman's bed."

Zachary assured her that he hadn't been in love with Lucinda for as long as he could remember. They had hardly ever made love in that bed, hardly even touched in that bed. The entire romantic part of their marriage had taken place in the first two years, when they were in the Peace Corps in India. "We stayed together for the kids," he told her. "I knew it was over," he said, "when she moved to pillow 4."

The king-size bed had four pillows, which Meg and Zachary referred to affectionately as pillows 1, 2, 3, and 4. Their bodies always lay close, on pillows 2 and 3, though at times Meg felt as if she might teeter onto the edge of pillow 4 and float away. In the back of her mind, she told herself, when the time was right, they'd get a smaller brass bed where there'd be no danger of drifting onto the pillows at the extremes, then off into the world.

"With you," he said, "it is different. You're easier to talk to. I can get close to you. We really are friends."

She'd met Zachary on a commuter train riding into Manhattan a month after he'd signed his divorce papers. She loaned him her business section. They met again on the train going home that night and from then on rode the train together. It took him a week to ask her to dinner. "I've just gotten out of something," he told her. "I can't rush right in."

She wasn't in a hurry either. Her marriage had ended a year before. A terrible, bitter ending in which her ex-husband and she called each other names neither could believe. How could people sink this low. She'd taken a vow and been alone for a year. She'd learned to enjoy living out of the city, spending Sundays taking walks in the woods. But soon Zachary and Meg were taking autumnal walks, buying baskets of apples upstate. They carved pumpkins like kids. Still they took it slowly. They didn't hop into bed. They spent weeks kissing in movie theaters, dancing close at clubs. They dreamed of each other in their separate beds. It was two months before they made love. They'd been seeing each other over a year before Meg moved in.

Zachary's son, Bennett, thought there was a spirit in his room that wanted to destroy him. Bennett was sixteen and he had a crucifix in his ear. He sang in a rock band called the Retards that played bar mitzvahs and school dances. He took the crucifix out when he played the bar mitzvahs but thought for now that the crucifix would keep the spirit away. He was concerned about what would happen when its power wore off. One night over dinner he said he could hear the spirit rumbling through his closet. "I think it likes my clothes," he said.

Bennett lived half the week with Lucinda and half the week with Zachary. Their daughter, Tracy, lived the opposite half of the week with each parent. It was what the kids wanted. "We each want all your attention," they said.

Meg found the arrangement tedious. Zachary and she had no time to themselves. There was always an adolescent around, always the bass of heavy metal and the ringing of phones. But Zachary said, "I'm a package. Take it or leave it." And Meg had replied, "I'll take it."

While Zachary wondered if Bennett was on drugs, because of the spirit, which he'd named Tronka, in his room, Meg was on Bennett's side. She wasn't sure what it was but at night she felt things. A movement, a trembling. She woke to the pounding of hooves, of things gone wild. When Bennett complained about the rumbling, Meg would say, Yes, I've heard it too.

Meg called a decorator. Her name was Lizzie and when she came over, Lizzie handed Meg her card. It read, "A rainbow in every room."

"A rainbow?" Meg asked, concerned.

Lizzie laughed. She was a slightly anorexic woman with limp brown hair and an extremely nervous manner. "It just means if you want a purple ceiling, I'll give you a purple ceiling. But I'll also give you mango throw pillows. If you want a turquoise floor, I'll give you a turquoise floor, but with lemon yellow chairs."

"Oh," Meg said, wondering if this was a good or bad sign.

"I believe in color. Fuchsia, tangerine, chartreuse. Lots of it. Brightness. And I can work around anything."

"Anything?"

Lizzie smiled smugly. "Anything!"

Meg directed her to the kitchen. "Can you work around this?"

Lizzie skipped only a beat. "No problem," she said, her mouth slightly agape before the wall. "I mean, if this is what we've got to work with, we'll make it work. I say we bring more color into the kitchen. More reds and yellows. Pick up what's in the mural. Oranges. And sea green." She wanted to look at the rest of the house.

"I see," she said, opening the closet that contained Lucinda's things. "This is what I call a house in transition. A family in flux." Downstairs Meg watched as Lizzie, a large, frail woman who reminded her of a twig about to snap, shoved the sofa with a bony hip. "It's nailed down," Meg said. Lizzie looked at the sofa in disdain. She made a note on her pad. They wandered back into the kitchen.

"How do you get along with your stepchildren, Mrs. . . . ?"

"Miss," Meg said. "We aren't married."

"Uh-huh." Lizzie made a note. "Do the children mind your redoing the house?"

"Well, we hadn't exactly . . ."

"Which child do you feel closer to? The boy or the girl?"

"Oh, the girl. I don't know. There are good things with each one."

"And you and Mr. Payne, are you very close . . . ?" Her lips trembled as she spoke.

"Excuse me, but what does this have to do with decorating?"

"Oh, everything." Lizzie ran a nervous hand through her hair. "You'd be surprised. The whole family dynamic is the decorator's responsibility. The way you all integrate with one another—it all has to do with my big scheme. It's not just throw pillows and wall hangings, you know." Her eyes scanned the wall. They stopped at the inscription, which read, "To Zachary, Lucinda, Tracy, and Bennett in peace and love, Mona."

"Lucinda?"

"The Ex." They both gazed, transfixed for a moment by the wall. "I can't do anything about that."

"Maybe you could just paint her name out," Lizzie said. "Stick your name in."

That night the heat rose, the boiler churned even though they'd lowered it. Bennett came downstairs twice, shouting, "Hey, Dad, quit turning the heat up." And Zachary shouted back how he'd just turned it down. The house creaked like a lonely cat and Meg felt the dark coupling of objects in the night—toaster to blender, chair to table. Appliances stirred. In the morning she woke as if she had not slept at all.

Meg hired Lizzie and the process began. The long-haired brown rug that lay like a dead animal on the floor was pulled out, the floors buffed smooth. The bright architectural lights that made the bed more a place for police investigation than lovemaking were removed and soft amber spots installed. New blue-green carpet was laid and with the amber spots, the bed looked like a raft, drifting on a gentle sea. The nailed-down

furniture was unnailed, the walls painted off-white. An ob-
structing wall in the living room knocked out. Light came in.

Late at night in the construction site that was to be their
home, the phone would ring. "Zachary, please," Lucinda
would say, and then Meg could hear her scream. "Your son has
blond streaks running through his hair. He's becoming a fairy, a
creep."

One night rather sleepily they were making love when the
phone rang. "Don't get it," Meg said. "She'll call back."

"I have children," Zachary reminded her, as if she had forgotten.

"I hope I'm not disturbing you," Lucinda said. "I just called
to say that it's one in the morning and your daughter has not
come home."

Zachary went over to calm her down. Then he found Tracy at
a friend's and took her back to her mother's to discuss her truant
behavior. Tracy had a new hole in the top of her ear and a pink
feather dangling from it. When he came home, he ate a DoveBar
and watched a late-night horror movie on cable. Bennett came
into the bedroom, where Meg sat alone. "What's up with the
oral sturgeon?" This was how he referred to his oral surgeon
father who liked to fish. Actually Zachary was renowned for the
invention of a movable plastic replacement for the human jaw,
and he traveled all over the world, presenting his invention.
"He's concerned about your sister, that's all," Meg said.

"I was gonna talk to him about the thing in my room, you
know, Tronka, but maybe this isn't a good time."

"Maybe not."

She went downstairs and saw Zachary taking out a box of bills he'd been putting off paying since they'd begun seeing one another. "Zachary," she called from upstairs, "don't you want to come to bed?"

"I think I'll read," he said. "Don't wait up for me."

It was morning when his body eased its way into bed and Meg reached for his hand. But he was too far away to find. She sat up and found him hovering close to pillow 1. "What is this? You come to bed at five in the morning and don't even kiss me good night."

"I didn't want to wake you," he said.

"Next time wake me."

In the morning as Meg had her coffee, she noticed that the sun in the mural had slipped behind a cloud. The sunflowers had turned away from the sun. She was about to mention it when Zachary bent down and kissed her. "I'm sorry," he said. "About last night. I've had so much on my mind lately. The kids and all."

"Oh," she said. "I understand. It's all right." When she looked back at the wall, the sun had returned as if it had never gone away.

Meg got some cartons from the store and began to pack away Lucinda's things. First she went to the closet near pillow 4 and took out Lucinda's dresses and skirts, her shirts and sweaters. Meg put them into neat piles on the bed. Then she took out the shoes and from another closet the coats and underwear.

She took out the kaftans and dashikis, the leftover floral prints. The peasant skirts, the suede shoes, the lace-up boots, the cowgirl jackets. She laughed as she folded them on the bed. How could anyone have dressed this way, she asked herself. But instead of packing, she began to put the clothes on. She put on a purple halter top and an embroidered Mexican shirt with puffy sleeves. A bulky alpine sweater, boots, a jacket. She dressed herself in layer after layer.

Lucinda was an ornithologist, an expert in the language of birds. Zachary had told her this. Birds, he said, spoke in dialects, and they had intonations that were as distinct as those of people from the north and the south. Whisper, nuance, secret murmurings. Lucinda knew them all. An educated bird could be told from an illiterate, a wise from a stupid, a cosmopolitan from a hick, a savage from a lamb. Her specialty was owls. Those creatures of the night, princes of darkness. Lucinda had journeyed, before the kids were born, to the wilds of Peru, the backwoods of Wisconsin, just to glimpse a snowy white.

Meg put on the clothes and stood before the mirror. She was thrilled when the peasant skirts fastened around her waist, when the pants zipped, the blouses buttoned. She was amazed at their eerie fit. She told herself, ''I'll keep these clothes. I'll wear them.'' But she packed them. It took hours. The packing, the labeling—shoes, floral-print blouses, Guatemalan sashes— but when she was done, Meg congratulated herself. There, it's over, she said. She's gone.

A few weeks later, Zachary had to go to Nairobi for a two-day conference to present his jaw. Meg didn't mind having time to herself. She liked to sit up in the middle of the bed reading as if she were queen of a small republic. Or she'd review the checklist of decorating changes she'd made, of the new ones she wanted to incorporate into her scheme. She looked over the list often because sometimes she had no idea what changes she'd made. At times she thought that nothing was different at all.

One evening Bennett walked into her room. A razor blade hung from around his neck, his hair had blue streaks running along the sides. "My parents aren't my parents," he said.

She sat up, closing the book. "Of course they're your parents, Bennett."

"I read a story once," he told her, "about these parents who were replaced by robots of parents. Sometimes I think that's what happened to my parents. Like extraterrestrials live in their bodies. Like they're not there at all."

"Have you tried telling them?" she said, suddenly concerned.

"The thing in my room, Tronka, I think that's my real parents. These people are from another place."

"Have you tried being open with them?" Meg felt oddly happy that Bennett had chosen her to confide in.

"Oh, they wouldn't listen to me at all. They'd just say, You're nuts, kid, see a shrink. There's no sense telling them a thing."

Later, as she drifted to sleep, the phone rang. A voice crackled at her from thousands of miles away. "I can't talk," he said. "I'm in a terrible rush."

Meg stared at the receiver in the darkened room. "You call from halfway around the world to say you can't talk?"

"I just want to make sure everything's all right."

"Everything's fine," she said. Then added softly, "We miss you, darling."

"Miss you too, honey," he replied. "Gotta run."

Meg went downstairs to make herself a cup of tea. As the water boiled she glanced at the wall. The Aztec temples shimmered, the pyramids stood high. But in a corner a woman wept on an unmade bed. A man about to leave stood faceless in a doorway.

When Zachary returned from Nairobi, Meg followed him around the house. "Please," she said, "let me paint the wall. If I could just paint it, I think I could live here as if this were my house."

Zachary sighed, bored with all of it now. "It would break Mona's heart," he said.

"I don't even know Mona," she cried. "I don't care about Mona."

"It would break her heart," Zachary said.

So break my heart then, she thought, but instead she said, "You were unfaithful to Lucinda, weren't you? You saw other women and she knew."

Zachary looked at her stunned. "Who told you that?" he asked. "How do you know?"

Lizzie came by to check on the construction and saw that it was going well, but Meg was dejected. "It's not working," she said. "It still feels the same. I mean, there's more light. The furniture's unnailed. But it's still her house. It's their house."

Lizzie listened, a kind look on her face. "Let me just ask you one more thing. I can work around anything. . . . I really can . . ." They were walking back downstairs and she hesitated, leaning closer to Meg as if she were about to whisper a very big secret. "But have you considered moving?"

That night they lay in bed, reading, the soft amber lights Meg had installed warming their faces. She looked at him. He had such gentle eyes, such long, strong hands. She loved his hands. Loved the way they turned the pages of books, they chopped vegetables. Loved the way they glided over her body when he felt like making love, which she was beginning to notice wasn't that often. At least not when they were in the house. When they went away for weekends to country inns or on business trips, he hardly took his hands off her. Or when the kids weren't around, they made love on the new carpeting or in the TV room on the new sofa. But in this bed, though it had happened slowly, almost imperceptibly, they made love less and less.

"I think we should move," she said to Zachary that night in bed. "The decorator thinks so as well."

"Oh, I think we'll do fine here," Zachary said. "A little more paint, a few more things. You'll see."

"But, look, could we just think about it?"

"I don't want the kids to have to make a big change at this point in their lives. You know, they've been through so much."

"We wouldn't have to move far."

He leaned over and kissed her, put his mouth to her ear. "Let's change the subject," he said.

"Then let me paint it," she pleaded. "Let me paint the wall."

The next night they went to a Chinese restaurant and ran into Mona. She was a large, flamboyant person who wore a Tibetan amulet around her neck. "Zachary," she said. "It's been so long . . ."

"This is Meg," Zachary said. "I've wanted you two to meet."

"Oh, you're the one who did the wall."

Mona waved her pudgy hand. "Oh, that thing?" She stared at Zachary, scolding him with her finger. "Is that still up? That's from an old cycle. Zachary, you should get rid of it. Get a fresh start."

First Meg photographed the wall as a record for Mona.

Then one weekend, when Zachary had gone fishing, she bought the white acrylic paint. With a sweep of the brush, the Aztec empire came down. Next she took out the lightning bolt and half the angel's wing. She wiped out the Indian nations, several animals on the endangered species list, a significant chunk of tropical rain forest, and assorted rare birds. She let it dry and then applied the second coat. But later that evening she saw that the paint barely covered the wall and the images continued to shine through. Meg phoned Lizzie. "Try yellow paint," she said.

"I don't want a yellow kitchen," Meg said.

"You can paint white over it," Lizzie advised.

Meg had a plan for the kitchen wall. She and Zachary would go out to the country and buy baskets, dried flowers, old prints of flowers and birds. They'd make a country kitchen for themselves. On Sunday morning she bought yellow paint and tried two coats but the wall still shone through.

She called Lizzie again. "What about black?" Lizzie said. "Black is very chic. Can you live in a black kitchen?"

"Black?"

"Well, if yellow doesn't cover it. After all, Bloomingdale's is black. It's stylish."

"It's a kitchen."

Meg was contemplating going out to buy black paint when the doorbell rang. A woman stood there in a soft pink angora sweater and brown slacks. Her hair was pulled back in a bun. She looked like the kind of person who would be handing out *The Watchtower* or collecting for the retired firemen's fund. "I've come for my things," Lucinda said. "I hope you don't mind."

Then she walked into the rooms that had once been her home. She looked at the light coming in, the new sofas and chairs, the tables against the wall. "You've made some changes, I see," Lucinda said.

"Yes." Meg spoke cautiously.

"You've unnailed everything."

"Yes." Meg was pleased she'd noticed. "Why did you nail it all down?"

"To keep it from moving," Lucinda said.

Meg cast a nervous glance around the room. "It was moving?"

"No," Lucinda said, "but everything else was."

They went down to the basement, where Meg had put her things. Lucinda appreciated the fact that Meg had folded her clothes, stored them carefully away. "It was nice of you to do this," Lucinda said. Meg was surprised at how kind she seemed. They carried the boxes outside and Meg helped put them in the car. The last time Lucinda walked through the house, she went into the kitchen. She glanced at the wall. Then she gave Meg an odd look and Meg couldn't tell if it was anger or praise. When they put the last box into the car, Lucinda said, "Thank you." Then added as an afterthought, "And good luck." Meg went back into the house. From the living room window she watched Lucinda sit in her car, head resting on the wheel, staring at the house. It was a long time before she drove away.

Then Meg went back to the kitchen. With one more coat of yellow paint, the wall was done.

When Zachary came home, he kissed her on the cheek, then carried the fish he'd caught into the kitchen, where he stood staring at the yellow wall, a blank look on his face. "It's your favorite color," Meg said.

"What have you done?" he asked, his body trembling. "What have you done?" Then he said nothing. All through dinner he was silent. That night it was a long time before he came to bed. When he finally did, he turned his back to her, his head on pillow 1. "Zachary," she said, "we can scrape the paint off if it matters that much to you."

"I needed it, Meg," was all he would say. "I needed that wall."

Beside him Meg tried to sleep, wondering when the gentle curves of their arms had changed to the harsh bend of spines. This night even their backs didn't touch. Still, Meg felt herself press against something hard. But when she turned there was nothing there. She lay awake, listening to the rumblings. Craters exploding, animals trying to claw their way out. The earth split; paint chipped. Downstairs the wall pulsed like a heart.

Slice of Life

ennie's Leaning Tower of Pizza—the original one in the Westfield Mall, and not the five chains Bennie's now got all over Orange County—is where I work five nights a week and Saturday afternoon. I've worked here for a long time and what began as a part-time kind of thing is starting to turn into my life. Of course, I've got other plans. When I get out of high school, which should be in another few years at the rate I'm going, I want to open a small retail store. Maybe video rentals off the Coast Highway.

For now I toss. My girlfriend, Sue, does the toppings. We've been going out since our surfboards collided on Huntington Beach two summers ago and I got her her job here. I toss and she chops. We didn't plan it this way, but it just kind of happened. Sue is good with the clean, swift strokes. She raises a knife in her suntanned hand and brings it down hard. Her wide hips and her long dishwater-blond hair sway like she's dancing. She can get rid of a mushroom or a green pepper the way a magician gets rid of a white rabbit. I'm better with dough. I know how to pound to make it pliable, how to get it spinning on the tips of my fingers until it's going like a top. And then I toss, higher and higher. I am not good at everything I do, but I'm proud of the few things I do well, and tossing pizza is one of them.

We make all kinds of pizzas here and some that even seem kind of strange, like pizzas with broccoli or melted goat cheese. And then we've got your average sausage and cheese, mushroom and anchovy. Some of them have names like the Sophia Loren with its big dark circles of pepperoni and the Al Capone with lots of anchovy, and the Joe DiMaggio, which is all veggie. Bennie gave them their names, don't ask me why.

I know most of the people who come here. Mr. Schultz comes in on Tuesday nights. He was my math teacher for umpteen years until he gave up on me. Mr. Schultz always orders a small Joe DiMaggio and always tells me how this is his wife's night to play cards with the girls. He seems sad when he tells me this and my mom says it's because everyone in town knows that there's no card game on Tuesday nights and his wife's having an affair with the soccer coach.

The O'Sullivans come in every Wednesday when we've got giants for the price of mediums and they always order the same thing, the Slice of Life. They've got three boys—Buddy, Oscar, and Scott. Oscar can't move his arms or legs. That is, they kind of just flop around and his head bobs in a funny way too. I can't quite describe it, but it's like Oscar's made of Play-Doh. I always bring the pizza to them myself because I like the way Oscar's mouth shapes itself into words that his mother translates for me as thank you. I give Oscar a free Coke when he says thank you because I know what a difficult thing it is for a kid like him to say.

I don't really know what's in the Slice of Life, but I know that it's got everything, plus something else. It's the something else I can't describe. Bennie says with a snicker it's a family secret, an ingredient handed down by the ancestors from the old country. I always ask if it's some kind of hash, but Bennie just laughs. He says it's a combination of things.

My mom comes in sometimes and she always wants a small plain cheese, which I tell her is the dumbest thing, but she says a haircut that looks like the tributaries of the Amazon with little rivers and canals running through it is also pretty dumb, so to each his own. I don't argue with that. Mom comes in more now since Dad stopped coming. He used to come a lot, but it dwindled to less and less, like those letters I used to get from a pen pal overseas.

My dad's got this funny way of doing things. He always has to know where we are, but we can't know where he is. He says he's not a gunrunner or involved with the CIA. He's just a very private person and needs his space. Before they split, my mom didn't complain much about this in front of us. But now, especially when his payments are late, she says he's involved with the mob and they're going to cement and deep-six him one of these days.

One night Sue and I are in the back and I've got her pressed against the butcher block. She's a big woman, strong as a horse, and I'm drawn to her the way I was to Amazons as a boy. I'm running my flour-coated hands up and down her arms until I can see the tattoo of a unicorn on her shoulder. When I first fell in love with Sue, it was for her tough walk and her unicorn tattoo. She starts moaning. "Let's close up and get out of here," she says just as my dad walks in. I pull away from Sue fast as if someone's come to rob the store and she says, "Hey, what's wrong?" He was never one to show up at good times and this is another instance. Where are you when I got expelled? I want to shout. When I fell off my motorcycle last year? Instead I say, "What'll it be?" I keep my hands under the counter so he can't see them trembling. It takes a moment for me to notice that he's got a girl with him, a small blond number who looks like his stenographer, if he ever needed a stenographer. They both have tans and some of her skin is peeling off her face. My dad's got his Hawaiian shirt unbuttoned and a few gold chains around his neck. "A medium cheese with half sausage, half mushroom, right, Marlene?"

Marlene just nods and smiles dumbly at me as if I really only am a pizza chef to this man. "So, Dad," I say emphatically, "how about a Coke or a nice root beer?"

"You've got a new haircut, I see."

"It's the latest," I tell him, turning so he can see the lines zigzagging, made by the tiniest razor in the world. "The California special, it's called."

I take longer than I need with their pizza. I make sure the dough is perfect, the edge fluted in just the right way. I arrange the sausage in a special swirl. Put the chopped mushrooms in a nice moon-shaped arrangement. I put it in on a slow bake and watch as my dad holds Marlene's hands as they sit by the window. He says things to her and she laughs, each time putting her hand across her face to cover her mouth until I realize she's wearing braces, wired teeth. This, I tell myself, from the man who spawned me.

I don't really hate him, but I can't say that I like him much either. I never did. The thing about my dad was you never knew what he'd do next. One minute we'd be washing salad in the kitchen. Next moment he'd slam me into a wall. One night at dinner we were all sitting around laughing. Next minute he throws a Coke in my face.

He used to take me out to learn things like golf. He'd put down a ball and say, "Look, kid, here's a ball. Now you hit it." Then I'd hack at it and miss until he'd take the club out of my hand and hit a long smooth drive. "See, kid," he'd say. "Any idiot can hit a nice drive." My mom said that one day when I was just a little kid and we were at a swimming pool, he said, "Well, time you learn how to swim." And he tossed me in. I don't remember any of this, but she said she had to dive in after me and I gagged for an hour.

My mom told me this just after she threw him out. She'd had a tough time with men, my mom. The guy before my dad was an actor who on his way to the wedding drove past the church and just kept going. At least my dad made it to the ceremony. She said she could have lived with him being unfaithful and not paying bills. What she couldn't live with was the things he did to me.

My girlfriend, Sue, tries to understand. Sue actually comes from a happy home where everyone gives each other presents for no reason at all and the hallway is filled with pictures of smiling relatives. She had an easy life until one day her twin choked to death at the dinner table. He was fraternal, so she never felt as if half of her had died, but she's never felt quite right after that either.

It's the O'Sullivans' night to show up, but so far they haven't. They weren't here the week before either, which I found strange since they've been every Wednesday since I started. I am beginning to think something is wrong, when I realize my dad's pizza is ready and it's smelling very done.

The crust is a little burnt and I say to myself without him saying a word to me, Can't you do anything right? If there's a wrong way to do it, do you have to find it?

I'm about to take the pizza to them when Sue grabs me by the arm. "Relax," she says. "He can't do a thing to you now." Wanta bet, I think of saying.

I give them their cheese with half sausage, half mushroom, and Marlene asks for a fork. I watch as she picks off every mushroom, one by one, moving them into a little pile by the side of her plate, like a squirrel hoarding its nuts. "Is something wrong?" I ask. "Would you rather have plain cheese?"

Marlene just smiles and shakes her head. "I like to save the best for last," she says, winking at my father. I understand that this is some joke between them, something I don't want to know about.

My dad chews carefully on his sausage. "Sit down, son," he says. "Looks like business is slow. Sit down. I want to talk to you." I don't want to sit down and I'm not sure I want to talk to him, but Sue nods for me to go ahead. "I can handle anything that comes in," she says. I'm hesitating, but just then Mr. Platsburg comes in. I can't stand Mr. Platsburg, because he always comes in and asks for a giant with everything, then he says just hold the anchovies, the sausage, the extra garlic, and the peppers. And I always say, Mr. Platsburg, why don't you just order an extra cheese and veggie, no peppers, but not Mr. Platsburg. It's always the giant everything and what to hold for him.

"Marlene and I are involved in a small business venture."

"Oh, yeah?" I say, giving the diamond in my ear a twirl.

"We were thinking of opening a small beauty parlor and thought maybe you'd like to come in on it. You've got a stable income, some money saved."

"Oh, yeah?" I run my hands through my hair. Then I don't say anything for a while. I just look at him, then at her, then back at him. My dad is waiting, poised, and I am pleased that I am keeping him waiting. Once he kept me waiting. I'd done something wrong at school and the principal called my dad. I don't know why he didn't call my mom, but he got my dad and he told me to go home and wait for him. I did that. I was maybe eight years old and I tried to do what I was told. I sat in a room and waited until he came home. Then he tied me to a chair. "You don't wanta go to school?" he said. "I'll give you a reason not to wanta go to school." And he shaved off my hair. I don't know why. It wasn't the style like it is now and I just sat there watching as my hair fell off my head in thick tufts.

"So we were thinking maybe you'd like to put a little of your savings into our project . . ." I could read right through this one. He'd lost in some two-bit card game and somebody was going to get him if he didn't come up with a thousand or so.

I am overcome with this desire to pound my father's face, then toss him into the air. I imagine myself twirling him on the tips of my fingers. I am about to pull my arm back and do this when my mom walks in with a look in her eyes like she's breathing fire. She stares at my dad and Marlene. "Whatever he wants, Brian," she says to me, but she never takes her eyes off them, "don't listen. Whatever he asks for," she says, "say no."

"Ginnie," he says with a half-cocked smile, "I just came to see my boy."

"He's doing fine without you seeing him." My mother is a tiny woman, not one to raise her voice, but she's acting like she's ready to go two or three rounds. "You visit him again, I'll get a court order." She turns to me. "I was driving by. I saw him sitting here. You okay?"

"Yeah, I'm okay."

"Gimme a slice to go," she says to Sue. "Don't listen to a word he says." Leaning against the counter but never taking her eyes off my dad, she takes her slice on its greasy slip of waxed paper. "I'll be home. If you need me, call," and she's gone.

It's not long before they get up to leave. "Now, listen, Brian," my father says. "Are you sure you can't loan your old man a little?"

"I'm sure. You know, Sue and me, we're thinking of getting married." I glance at Sue, whose eyes roll, then smile complacently at my dad. "But the pizza, Dad, it's on me." As they leave, I watch my father's back recede. I take aim at him, as if I've got a dart in my hand. It was the one game he actually taught me how to play. I think I'll never see him again. Or if I do, it'll be when I need him the least.

I'm thinking of putting out the CLOSED sign, taking Sue out back, laying her across the butcher block table, and having my way, when the O'Sullivans come in. They seem different somehow and it takes me a while to notice Oscar isn't with them. It's just Buddy and Scott and the parents. Mrs. O'Sullivan looks about ten years older and I'm wondering what I should say when she looks up at me. "The usual, Brian," she says as if nothing's wrong. "Just give us the usual."

I make them a Slice of Life. I order the vegetables and pepperoni in a beautiful swirl like a flower unfolding. The jar with the special ingredients is almost empty. Bennie always fills the jar, but I know he keeps a sack in the back, so I go into the storage room and find it. I reach into the large burlap sack and pull out a slip of paper. It reads: parsley, basil, oregano, thyme.

I take a fistful of the ingredients in my hands and sniff it. Is this it? I ask myself, looking back at the slip. Could this be all?

I let the O'Sullivans sit there, munching on their crust, as we close up. Sue hardly says a word as she puts the remnants of her choppings into Ziploc bags—mushrooms, green peppers, sausage—for tomorrow's round. I scrub the counters clean. When they get up to leave, Mr. O'Sullivan comes over and clutches my hand. "Thank you, Brian. You have been very kind."

We lock up late. Some nights after work we bowl a few and some nights we go to a club nearby, but this night I want to take a ride near Pelican Point. "Let's head for the beach," I say. We get in the car and drive. We drive until we spot the moon, resting over the Pacific, round and orange and perfect. I pull into a sandy ditch and for a few moments stare at the sky. Then I cannot resist, I burst into song. "When the moona hits your eyes like a bigga pizza pie, dat's amore . . ."

Sue puts her fingers across my lips. "Shush," she says, "let's just be quiet for a while."

As we sit, I shape my fist into a round, even ball and point it straight at the moon as if I could smash right through the windshield and blot out the light. Sue must know what I'm thinking, because she reaches across and pulls me to her chest. I bury my face against her shoulder at the place where the unicorn must be. She dusts my hair. "You're covered with flour," she laughs, and I let her knead me in her hands like dough.

THE
Lure

he first time Ben asked Laurel to fly to Wisconsin
with him to spend a week with his father, Laurel
said no. She wasn't partial to fathers. During the
sixties Laurel's father left her mother for a famous activist.
Laurel had tried to stay away from fathers ever since. While Ben
went home to visit his father, Laurel traveled through Europe
with a friend on a Eurail pass for two weeks. She came back
from Europe with snapshots of dozens of Gothic cathedrals, dull
gray and stately, which had withstood many centuries. Ben returned with glowing reports of an old timber lodge with a huge

fireplace set on the shore of Lake Michigan. Reports of a million berries on the shrubs in the woods, of long walks to pick them.

"So, how was Martha?" Laurel asked after he finished telling her about the house. Ben could go on for hours talking about the house, barely mentioning his father and never mentioning Martha. Two years after his mother died, Ben's father married a beautiful woman named Martha.

"She's all right," Ben replied. "They fight a lot."

"That doesn't mean they're unhappy." Laurel actually was defending herself. She and Ben fought a lot as well.

"My parents never fought." He gave his pat reply. Laurel was a reporter for a mediocre New York newspaper and she'd learned a few things. She learned that what gets left out is often more interesting than what gets put in. She looked at Ben. His fingers tugged at his thin, sandy hair, a gesture Laurel knew meant he didn't want to talk about something.

He didn't want to talk about how he used to sit on his hands to prevent himself from putting them tightly around Martha's throat. Ben passed time when he was younger imagining all the terrible accidents that could happen to Martha in the course of the day. Sometimes he waited for the phone to ring with the bad news that never came.

Ben began waiting for the bad news right after Harry married Martha. Harry met her in the pathology lab where they both worked. "You know," Ben said to Laurel once, "I think she was just waiting for Mom to die." It didn't do any good when

Laurel pointed out that they married two years later. "That was for appearances' sake," Ben always said.

After Ben's mother died, Harry took him fishing and camping alone for a month on Green Bay. Harry taught Ben all he knew about the different kinds of tackle, bait, and lures. He showed Ben how to bring a fish up from down deep and how to coax it out of a rocky place. He taught him how to pick a fly and cast in a stream. He taught him which plastic lures will snare a pike in the middle of the lake. At night Harry cooked the fish they'd caught in the day over an open fire. One night as Harry cooked, Ben saw two tears slide down his face and evaporate in the heat of the fire. Shortly after that trip, Harry met Martha. Ben hadn't been alone with his father again since he married her.

Ben didn't tell Laurel then, though he'd tell her later, that he felt as if he could choke Martha. But he did confide in her one night shortly after he returned that he saw his mother from time to time. Ben and Laurel were lying in bed together and he stroked her hair as he told her this. "Sometimes I'll be in the laundromat and I'll see her sorting my socks. Or in a restaurant, she'll be laughing at the next table."

A few days before she died from a hideous and extended illness, Ben woke in the night and found his mother standing in her nightgown at the foot of his bed. She said she was cold, so Ben pulled back the covers and made a comfortable place for her to lie down. She curled beside him like a lover, hugging him and shivering. In the morning when Ben woke, she was gone.

When he asked her what time she'd gotten up, his mother said she had no idea what he was talking about. She'd spent the entire night on the sofa in the den.

On Thanksgiving Laurel found herself in a plane flying with Ben to Green Bay. When Ben had told her they were going to Wisconsin for Thanksgiving, she'd said no, but Ben wasn't asking. He was telling. They sat in silence during most of the flight. They'd had a fight in the cab to the airport. They'd fought over the fact that Laurel didn't want to make this trip. She'd said to him in the cab, "I wish you hadn't said yes for me."

But his father had already made the reservations and had gotten tickets for the Packers game. "He didn't give me much choice," Ben replied.

Laurel sighed and wondered how she'd gotten herself into this mess. She didn't want to be involved in somebody's family. She didn't want to be involved with anyone in this way. Laurel met Ben through a friend of hers named Stefanie. Stefanie worked on the police blotter and one day Laurel told her she wanted to meet a man. So a week later Stefanie said, "I've got a great guy for you. Handsome, sexy, smart, talented, runs his own graphic design studio, loves to travel . . ."

"What's wrong with him?" Laurel asked.

Stefanie had hesitated. "He doesn't get involved." It seemed he'd been Stefanie's boyfriend for a long time and finally she gave up trying. When Stefanie gave Ben Laurel's number, he wasn't interested at first. But then he noticed that they both had a 260 telephone exchange which meant that if they started seeing one another, he could walk home in the morning.

It began as a matter of convenience. Then one morning as Ben was buttoning his shirt, he told Laurel, "Listen, I think I better warn you. I don't get serious."

"Don't worry," Laurel had said. "I don't either."

From New York to Green Bay, Laurel played the scene over and over in her mind. She couldn't understand how they'd gone from that to this. She couldn't understand how he'd gotten her on to this plane.

Harry was a tall, elegant man, like Ben, only with silver hair that seemed to shimmer as he walked. Harry and Ben had the same soft brown eyes, the same wide smile. Harry was a research scientist until he retired a few years before. He had a vaccine named after him, Bancroft's serum, something he discovered that saved the lives of infants who had a mysterious, and now, thanks to the serum, nonexistent, disease.

Martha kissed Ben, who took it the way a corporal might take a command from his immediate superior. Martha and Laurel shook hands, but then Martha, as if in an afterthought, leaned over and kissed Laurel as well. Martha was fifty-five but she didn't look forty. Laurel expected that. What she didn't expect was that Martha would look like the picture of Ben's mother he kept on his dresser and she wondered why he'd never mentioned it before.

When they got into the car, Martha said, "Shall we take them for a ride around town first? I want to show Laurel our little shops."

Harry shook his head. "They're only here for a few days. They don't need to shop. They can shop in New York."

"Oh, well, I just thought . . ."

Ben nudged Laurel slightly, making certain she didn't miss this minor point. But Harry took the route through town anyway. He drove down Main Street and helped as Martha pointed out the boutiques, the small grocers, the fish and tackle shop. Then they drove home. The house was a few miles outside of town and it sat right on the bluff overlooking Lake Michigan. The Bancrofts had their own beach. The house was an old hunting lodge that Harry and Martha bought a few years before when he decided to give up his teaching post in Madison. As they drove up, Martha said, "Well, this is our little cottage."

They walked into the main room, a large, two-story living room with a moose head staring down at them from above the mantel. The moose had glassy, maudlin eyes. Laurel thought the moose had as much business being here as she did. On the wall were paintings, the kind a child had obviously done. Paintings of fish and birds and the lake. There were bright-colored paintings of dunes, sloping gently to the sea, of starfish and whales, swimming with lake trout, mixed with coral.

Then there were other paintings that seemed dark, with strange figures hovering overhead like ghosts in the air. In one painting there was a tidal wave with a boy, facing the wall of water with fish being flung at him from the wave. In another there was a rainbow-colored fish, struggling on a hook, blood gushing from a gash in its throat, its eyes bursting from its head. The fish stared out of the painting, and seemed to be looking as if to ask some question.

Ben, noticing Laurel looking at the paintings, said, "I can't believe he hasn't gotten rid of these." He pointed to himself. "From my early fish period."

Martha fluttered around, puffing up pillows, saying things like, "I bet you guys are starved. Let me just stick some cheese puffs into the oven." But Harry said, "C'mon now, dear. Show them upstairs." Martha frowned, but obeyed, leading them up the staircase into the bedroom. The bedroom had an old brass bed which Laurel felt certain would squeak. "Just make yourself comfortable," Martha said, patting the crazy quilt. "You do want to be in the same room, don't you?"

Ben nodded and rolled his eyes. "Yes, we want to be in the same room." He winked at Laurel and she winked back but for a moment she thought it might be nice to be apart. Even though neither of them wanted to get involved, she found that they hadn't been apart, except for when he went to Wisconsin and she went to Europe, a single night. Lately her feelings for Ben had been muddled.

There were things about him she couldn't stand. His Hawaiian shirts, the punk haircuts he insisted upon, the way he left dishes in the sink and drank Ovaltine in the morning, that digital watch he was always setting. In the middle of an argument he'd set the clock and tell her how much more time she had to blow up. And his notion of true love, which was right out of a nineteenth-century novel—certainly not the kind of love people who live in a loft in lower Manhattan should be thinking about. He wanted that perfect mingling of the souls. He wanted two people to act as one.

Laurel acted at times like two people all by herself, Ben often commented. She'd thought about leaving him and occasionally told her sublettor to try and find something else. But in the end she'd stayed with him. She didn't know why. She couldn't explain it to him or to herself. It went beyond love. She knew that somewhere inside of them, they were alike. And, though she hated admitting this to anyone, let alone herself, she would be lost without him.

Harry and Martha uncorked a bottle of wine when Ben and Laurel came downstairs. Harry poured the wine and Martha ran in and out of the kitchen, checking the parsley potatoes, the rainbow trout. "I'll bet you caught it yourself, Dad," Ben said when he saw the fish frying in the kitchen.

"Naw," Harry said, rather shyly. "If you'd get here more often, maybe I'd catch my own."

Martha passed the cheese platter around. "Why don't you guys go off fishing. I'm sure we girls could amuse ourselves."

Laurel nodded. "I'm sure we could." But she couldn't imagine amusing herself while the men went off fishing.

To Laurel's surprise, dinner wasn't very good. The fish was overcooked. The potatoes uncooked. The spinach was too salty. "So." Harry turned to Ben. "You like running your own business?"

Ben had recently opened his own graphic design studio. "You know, I've got more clients than I can handle right now."

Harry nodded, listening carefully. "No more thoughts about painting again, huh?"

"I like what I'm doing," Ben replied, coldly.

"I don't blame you," Martha said. "I'd rather work with people around me any day.

Harry looked annoyed and said he was tired. "And you guys must be exhausted, no?" Everyone agreed that everyone was tired and right after the dishes, they headed upstairs.

Ben and Laurel crawled under the covers and Laurel said, "Will you hold me."

Ben yawned. "For a minute." They both tensed up. Laurel always wanted to be held longer than Ben wanted to hold her. But he reached out and pulled her close to him.

"I love you," Laurel whispered.

He kissed her on the forehead. "Me too." And he rolled over and went to sleep.

L aurel was up before Ben so she got dressed and went outside. When she got onto the beach, she saw Harry near the shore. He was dressed in fishing gear and on his hands and knees. In front of him were several boxes, filled with colored objects which Laurel saw as she approached. "Good morning," Laurel said to him. Then she stooped down and picked up a yellow plastic fish, something that looked like a bug with feathers. "What're these?"

"Oh, flies, lures. I thought I'd get my boxes ready, just in case."

"How come they're all different colors?"

Harry looked up at her slightly. "Well, each situation requires a different type of tackle. For instance, you don't catch a sturgeon with the same things you'd catch salmon with. You want to find the thing the fish thinks it knows. You fish with that." He explained to her how the flies looked like the bugs that come off the streams and how the lures look like the different fish. "In the lake you use lures. In the lake when you go out deep, you want something that'll shimmer like a minnow. You've gotta make the fish think you've got the real thing." Harry laughed. "You gotta fake the fish out. If you're gonna drag 'em up from the deep, you've gotta get the right lure."

"Sounds pretty complicated," Laurel said. It did sound complicated to her.

"No, it's just common sense."

Later that morning Harry made one of his famous breakfasts—cranberry pancakes, crisp bacon, orange juice, scrambled eggs, a huge pot of coffee. Laurel groaned when she saw all the food. "I won't have room for turkey."

"Oh," Martha said. "We're having goose and you've got lots of time between now and dinner."

"Why don't you kids go for a long walk on the beach," Harry suggested.

Laurel took the plate heaped with pancakes as Harry passed it to her. "I've got an idea. Why don't I help Martha get dinner and you guys go for a walk?" Laurel saw Ben smile at her.

But Harry shook his head. "Now don't be silly. You're on vacation. You should relax."

Fifteen steps led from the back of the Bancroft yard to the beach. Laurel and Ben climbed down slowly to walk on the sand. It was a cold, gray November day and they were bundled up. Ben held Laurel's hand as they walked. She felt a tension in his fingertips. "See what I mean? He just doesn't want to spend time with me. He'll find any excuse. He won't even take a walk."

"Well, you didn't really ask him, did you?"

Ben shook his head. "I don't have to ask him. I can tell. He'll always find excuses."

Laurel's ears were red and cold and she put her collar up. "Sounds like you've got your own set of excuses. Takes one to know one." Ben let go of her hand. He was irritated that she couldn't see the situation the way he saw it. He knew his father had been ignoring him for years. Laurel was also annoyed with Ben as she walked toward the water. Ben watched her walk away. Her auburn ponytail bobbed like a cork on the water. She was watching the gulls, skimming the surface of the water.

Ben caught up with her. "Mom used to love it here. She was crazy about the birds and the lake."

Laurel slipped her hand through Ben's arm. "I guess you miss her."

He wrapped his fingers around her fingers. "No," he spoke softly. "I miss him."

L ater they sat down to Thanksgiving dinner. Martha had set the table with an old lace tablecloth and real silver. She cooked a tremendous goose. Laurel felt as if all she'd done since arriving was eat. She didn't know how she'd make it through this meal. "I just love Thanksgiving," Martha said, fluttering around the table. "Just think, Harry. It's been eighteen years we've been doing this together. I don't know where all the time went."

Harry was carving but his face suddenly seemed distracted. He looked up at the ceiling as if listening for an animal on the roof. "Is it really that long?"

Martha continued to move around the table. "So, everyone has what they want, right? You know, I can't remember when I cooked a goose last. Goose is fatty. You have to cook it slowly."

"Mom always made turkey, didn't she, Dad?" Ben said.

His father thought for a moment. "I guess so. I guess she did make turkey."

"You don't like goose?" Martha asked Ben.

"Oh, I'm just used to having turkey, that's all."

"Well," Martha said, sitting down, "I thought we'd try something different for a change."

Ben shrugged. "I'm just not used to it."

Then Martha rose quickly and tossed her napkin down. "I forgot the cranberry Jell-O." Her voice was shrill and everyone stared at her.

Harry kept his eyes on the napkin she tossed down. "What is it, dear?" Harry followed her into the kitchen.

Laurel looked at Ben. His face was flushed. "What's going on?" she whispered.

"She can't stand it," Ben whispered back. "She can't stand it even if we mention her." But for some reason Laurel wasn't sure that that was what was bothering Martha.

The next afternoon Ben, Laurel, and Harry went to see Green Bay lose to Cleveland. Laurel sat between Ben and Harry and she rooted for Cleveland. They rooted for Green Bay. Laurel hadn't wanted to sit between them, but that was the way they sat down on the bleachers. Laurel went to the bathroom in the middle of the second quarter and stayed away almost until halftime, but Ben and Harry didn't close the space between them.

That evening after dinner, everyone drank cognac and sat around the table. Ben played a fairly good ragtime and Harry did a few numbers from the thirties. Then Ben played a medley of show tunes. Martha poured more cognac and leaned on

Ben's shoulder. When Ben played "Some Enchanted Evening," Martha sang into his ear, "You may see a stranger across a crowded room . . ." Her voice was gravelly and flat and she skimped on the high notes. She closed her eyes and let her body swing.

Harry wrinkled his nose at Ben, but Martha opened her eyes in time to see it. She stopped singing. "Is it that bad?" No one said a word. "Tell me, if it's that bad, I don't have to sing at all."

"Dear, this isn't a competition." He waved his hand at her. "I'm going to track down some more firewood." But when he went outside, Martha went upstairs. A little while later Harry came back in. His face was red and a white cloud came from his mouth. "This should make a nice fire." Then he looked around. "Where's Martha?" Ben pointed upstairs and Harry said, "Damn." He went up and didn't come back down again that evening.

When they got into bed later, Ben and Laurel had a fight. It was their first real fight in a while. Normally they just sulked away from each other, but tonight when they got into bed, Laurel felt as if she just had to make love and she was certain Ben would not want to. "Please, don't go to sleep. I need you." Laurel shook Ben, trying to convince him not to fall asleep.

"Not here. You can hear everything in this house. How about tomorrow night in New York?"

Laurel put her hand on his shoulders. "Please, please don't go to sleep. Please, I want to talk to you. Ben, I love you." Her fingers dug into his shoulders but she felt him drifting away from her, into that place where he could always hide.

He lay with his back to her. "Look, Laurel, I don't think this is what I want. Maybe you should move back to your apartment for a while."

"Then why did you bring me here? To sit at a football game between you and him. Is that all I'm here for?"

Ben groaned. "Would you please keep it down?"

"How can you possibly know what you want? You don't even try. You haven't even tried since I met you."

Suddenly Laurel was out of bed. She stood in her pink nightgown in the middle of a hooked rug in a patch of light, coming from the moon. She stood in that patch of light and Ben turned over onto his back.

She was crying and Ben just stared at her. He saw her standing there at the side of the bed, the light coming from the window through her pink nightgown. He saw her legs, her thighs, her breasts. He looked up at her hands, shielding her face and her disheveled hair, and she reminded him of another moment in his life, when he'd thought he'd seen his mother standing at the edge of his bed, just before she died. "Come here." He pulled the covers back and made a space for her to lie down. She was cold and shivering and he held her close. He kissed her gently on the forehead as she drifted to sleep.

But Ben couldn't sleep and after a little while he eased his way out of the bed. Leaving Laurel resting on the pillow, he slipped downstairs to get a drink of water. When he reached the first landing, he saw his father, sitting under a small lamp, reading from a journal on biochemistry. Ben wanted to go back into his room but his father had already seen him. "Hi there," Harry said. "Wanta beer?"

Ben said sure so Harry went and got two Heinekens. He popped them open and they sat down across from one another. "I had a fight with Laurel," Ben said, wondering why he said that.

Harry nodded. "The house isn't very soundproof." Harry took a long swig. "So, do you guys have plans?"

Ben was starting to feel uncomfortable. He felt as if he couldn't breathe and he wanted to go back upstairs. "No, we don't have plans. We fight too much."

"Nothing wrong with a good fight now and then. Martha and me, we fight sometimes, but I think it's better than keeping it all inside, the way your mother did."

The wind was howling outside and the house suddenly seemed colder to Ben. His father looked odd under the light of the Tensor lamp. Finally Ben whispered, "But you and Mom, you were so happy."

Harry shrugged. "Oh, I loved your mother, but I never felt close to her. Martha, she's my friend. We don't have any secrets." He finished his beer. "It's not the same as with your mother, of course. But in some ways it's better." He paused, as if expecting Ben to say something, but Ben could think of nothing to say. "Hey," his father put his hand on his knee, "why don't you guys stay a few extra days and go fishing with me?"

Ben shook his head and yawned. "We've gotta get back. I guess I'd better get some sleep now." His whole body trembled. He didn't know what else to say. His father got up too, stretched, and they climbed the stairs together. When they reached the landing, they paused. His father touched him on the shoulder. "Don't say I didn't ask." Then they went into their separate rooms.

In the morning Laurel got up first. She looked out the window. It was a clear, cool day, good for flying. The room was chilly and she dressed quickly. Ben reached out and grabbed her while she was dressing. He pulled her to him and kissed her on the neck. "Hey," she said to him, "what's gotten into you?"

When Laurel went downstairs, she saw Martha sitting with a cup of coffee, staring down at the beach. "Look at that bird," Martha said. "It must be hurt."

Laurel looked out and saw the gull, running around in circles. Its head seemed connected to its wing and it kept twisting and turning. Then it would flop down exhausted on the sand. Then begin again. Something protruded from the wing, like a piece of bone, and it seemed to be sticking through. The gull turned and ran frantically, then sank back into the sand again.

Ben and Harry had come down by this time and they went out to the railing above the beach to look. "Its wing looks broken," Ben said.

But Laurel saw the thin, silver-blue fish protruding from under the wing, the wire wrapped around the body. "It's tangled up in something."

Ben leaned further over the railing. "You're right. It's all tangled up.'' Harry thought of the thick, green gardener's gloves and the wire cutters and he headed for the garage. Laurel and Ben went down to the beach together. They bent over the gull as it shook with pain, its wing hooked to its neck, the neck hooked to the mouth. It had three hooks in it and the blue-silver fish was the lure it had tried to take in its mouth. ''Go tell my dad to hurry,'' Ben said.

Laurel ran up the steps. She wished she hadn't had any coffee on an empty stomach. She began to feel jittery and nauseous as she raced across the yard. She went into the house. ''She's taken a lure,'' Laurel said to Martha.

''Oh, how awful,'' Martha replied, handing Laurel a warm sweater. ''Put this on, dear.'' Laurel went into the garage, but Harry had already headed to the beach. She saw his head disappear as he descended the steps. She ran back to the railing to see if they needed anything from the house.

Ben and Harry had already put on the gardener's gloves and they were stooping over the bird. She watched from the railing above them while Ben held the gull as steadily as he could and his father, the doctor, snipped at the wires connecting the plastic sardine. After a few moments Harry tossed the sardine away. Ben and Harry, their hands entangled, worked on the hooks, squatting over the gull. In whispers they gave each other instructions. Laurel heard Ben say, ''Dad, I can't get this one out of her wing.'' She heard Harry reply, ''We'll have to give it a good yank.'' Then their voices faded and all Laurel could hear was the sound of the water.

Laurel was about to head down to join them when Martha,

who had come to the railing, caught her by the arm. "They seem to be making out well," Martha said, as she led Laurel by the arm back toward the house and into the kitchen. The two women stood by the sink, cracking eggs, with their eyes to the window, watching the horizon. After a few minutes, they saw the gull rise from the beach and fly shakily to a distant rock. It landed on the rock and flapped its wings several times. They kept their eyes on it until it flew away.

Ben convinced Laurel to stay a little longer so that he and Harry could go fishing. They came back with enough lake trout for dinner. The trout had sleek, rainbow bodies and Harry commented on how it was rare this time of year to be able to catch this many because the water was already turning cold and the fish had gone down deep.

Souvenirs

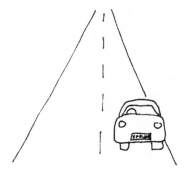

The winter my parents took us from the freezing suburbs of Chicago to Florida, I began to steal. It wasn't anything I'd intended, anything I had planned. It just happened that way. Every year we begged them to take us with them and every year they said no. In winter when the Illinois snow was piled in six-foot drifts and I could skate in the streets to school, my mother and father would get into their car, leaving us with Mini, the Italian woman who cleaned our house, or with our dreaded aunt Miranda, who raised children by the book, and head south for two weeks without us.

I watched them go. I'd place my nose against the window of the car and stare as my mother disappeared behind her own breath, steaming the glass first with kisses, then with admonishments, and finally with her shouts, pleading with whomever was in charge to take us away. Once I had to be pried off the car as if dry ice held me there.

Those two weeks without my parents were always unclear in my mind, foggy like my mother's image through the glass. What I found I remembered most wasn't what I'd done while they were gone, but where they'd been. They sent us cards from along the way. Year after year it was the same cards. Thoroughbred horses grazing on the bluegrass of Kentucky. Moss-covered manses from Georgia. And then from Florida a stream of oranges, thick upon the trees, aquatic birds, rising, a view of the sea, the generic alligator. The postcards came from places that had dream names to me—Chattanooga, Savannah, the Everglades. For the two weeks each winter that they were away and my brother Sam and I waded knee-deep in snow, I pictured my parents on islands named Sanibel or Paradise, surrounded by pink birds and lianas, alligators nipping at their heels.

Then they'd come home, two weeks later to the day. My mother always seemed exhausted, a bit subdued. She said the car trip made her tired. She stayed clear of the sun for it freckled her face and she seemed to return paler than when she'd gone, even though her black hair and white skin always made her look a bit like a ghost to me. Still, there was something about her that came back altered, at least for a time, as if she'd had a dream that she kept pondering for days on end. My father returned bronzed, golden, though much less relaxed than before he'd gone away, for bills had piled up, something had always gone wrong. He moved through the house like a bull, pounding on pipes, checking the things that hadn't been tended to while he was away. On the surface they returned much as they'd gone, yet I always felt something had transformed them, that during the annual journey to Florida something had happened that excluded my brother and me further from their world.

We wanted to know everything. We wanted to hear everything. But first the car had to be unpacked, things put away. Mail and messages had to be gone over and discussed. Then sometime in the evening my parents assembled us in the den, where my mother handed out the requisite gifts—a box of citrus fruit, the T-shirts we'd outgrow before it was warm enough to wear them, a bag of pearly, shiny shells, a pencil case, souvenirs.

Then my father would tell us about the trip. He wouldn't just tell us incidents. He would tell us everything that had happened to them—where they stopped, what they ate, who they met, what they saw. Their faces would light up as they talked of these things, the fatigue would leave their eyes, and I had a sense of what a wonderful time my parents had without us, how happy they were when they were away.

———

T he year when I turned thirteen and was on the brink of discovering boys and my brother, who was ten, had just joined a basketball league, my parents suddenly decided to take us with them. My mother, dressed in a flimsy nightgown, her hair piled on her head, came into my room one night as I was already tucked into bed. She patted my foot and I scooted over. "Well," she said, "how would you like to go with us this year?"

"Go with you?" I said. "Where?"—though I knew full well.

"Why, to Florida," she laughed with her head thrown back in a way I'd never seen her laugh before. Then she patted my leg again. "You've always wanted to come with us. Why wouldn't you like to come now?" I thought that because of my age, I had reached the point where I was old enough. Yet I'd also reached the point where I didn't really care. Already I was moving on to other things.

Later I passed my brother in the hall, where he was bouncing a basketball, which was strictly forbidden. "You don't want to go either?" I asked him. He just shook his head. "But, of course," I said, "we'll go." He nodded as he dribbled toward his room.

O ne frozen winter's day not long after that, I packed a swimsuit, some shorts, my summer dresses into a bag and we tossed our luggage into the trunk, but not before my father rearranged it so many times that finally my mother said,

"Dear, we're all going to the same place. What does it matter whose bag is on top of whose?"

My father did what he always did in those moments, which surprised me because this was supposed to be different, because we were going away. He pursed his lips, his eyes turned red. "Do you want to stay home? Do you want to forget about this trip? Then let me pack the car."

No one argued when he spoke like this. In the house we had learned how to drift off into our various directions. My brother to his hoop, me to my books, my mother into her sewing room, my father behind the newspaper and the television. But now we were to be stuffed for three days into this car and the reality seemed to be sinking in. In funereal silence, we took our seats, seats we would assume for the entire journey, never once vacillating. My father in the driver's seat, my mother in the passenger's. Me and Sam crammed into the back, his basketball between his legs, my mother's sewing and a small duffel of books and magazines which I'd flip through over the course of the next three days between mine.

We got onto the interstate and drove straight, only pausing at the oasis along the highway to eat or at a Holiday Inn to sleep, then back in the car again. Every few hours we stopped at a service center or convenience store, where we'd wolf down a hot dog or grab a Coke and a bag of chips. Then we were back on the highway again. Sometimes we squirmed or begged to be let out, but my father always said, "Just a little bit longer. I want to make Lexington by night." Legs bent, knees to chin, my brother and I stared blankly out the window as a dreary winter Midwestern landscape passed, waiting for the trip to begin.

At the Louisville oasis toward the end of our first day as we sat at a window table, peering down at a six-lane highway and miles of snow-covered farmland with miserable cattle dotting the fields, I turned to my parents and said, "When do we get to see the horses and the plantations? Where are all the birds?"

"Oh, they're not on the highway," my mother said. My mother was not very young then, having married late. She was in fact the age that I am now as I write. She had thick black hair, beautiful pale skin with freckles that I loved to poke at when I was a child. She hated many of the features of her body—her skin, her nose, her breasts—but I thought she was beautiful like a Renoir model. My father was handsome and older as well, with silver hair and dark skin.

"You want to get there, don't you?" My father spoke, an exasperated look in his eye.

"But all those cards you sent . . ."

"You want to see Florida, or don't you?" My father didn't always talk to me like this. It had only been in recent years. He used to come into my room every night and sing me a song and tell me a story. It was the way I went to sleep. He'd sing in his slightly discordant tenor voice "Count Your Blessings" or "Over the Rainbow." My mother would blow kisses from the doorway and say, "Did you catch it? Roses on your pillow." But my father sat at the edge of my bed and crooned.

"Oh," my mother laughed, "those cards." She ran her hand over her face as if trying to hide her shame. "We always bought them right here," pointing across the Louisville oasis.

At the newsstand where my mother bought the cards of the places she'd never been, an old woman was at the cash. She had no teeth and yellow fingers, a beanbag ashtray full of butts in front of her. Her sticky pink hair stood up high on her head. She smiled as I picked up candy, turned the postcard turnstile.

"Where you going, little girl?" she said in a raspy voice.

"Florida," I replied.

"Florida," she laughed. "Oh, yeah, Fountain of Youth. Can I come along?"

"There's not much room in the car," I said, almost taking her seriously.

Then I found what I thought I wanted. A plastic key chain with a thoroughbred racehorse dangling from it. The horse was jet black with white feet and had won the Derby several years back. He was on a stud farm somewhere in Kentucky, a place whose name I have forgotten, but I knew at the time that it wasn't far from the interstate where we drove. I had money, but as she rang up another customer, I tucked the key chain into my breast pocket. Feeling it safe there, I said good-bye to the old woman. "Have fun," she said. I kept the key chain for a long time until I had rubbed off all the information about the horse taped to the back—his name, his sire, the races he'd won, where he'd been put out to stud.

In the car as dusk settled and my mother dozed and my father drove intently, eyes set straight ahead, I showed my brother the key chain. I opened my palm and just held it as if it were a chalice, a piece of the Holy Shroud. He looked at it, then looked at me, his dark eyes widening. I put my finger over my lips. "I stole," I whispered. His eyes lit up for the first time on the trip.

Sam and I shared a room. There had been some debate about this, my mother suggesting that "the girls" sleep in the same room, but my father always used the same threat. "If you don't want to go," he'd say, "it's fine with me." So my mother deferred, though she worried about this. "Will you be all right, sharing a room with your brother?"

"It's all right, Mom. We'll be fine."

Each night we stayed in a Holiday Inn in a different-colored plaid room. Our first night out, the night I stole the key chain, my brother and I got a room that was orange and green. It had two queen-size beds and a big TV. I took the bed by the window and the TV, Sam got the one by the bathroom, because I was oldest and had the privileges that come with age. Once we were settled in our room, my brother said, "I want to see it. I want to see it again."

I handed him the key chain, the black horse standing proud, dangling below. "How'd you do it?"

"It was easy," I told him. "I just took it." I'd never stolen anything before, but I was surprised at just how easy it was. I, of course, had no cause to steal it. My parents would have given me anything I'd wanted. But already this was getting into my blood. "Just take things that don't matter; take what you don't need or care about." Already I found myself starting to sound like a petty thief. "Take little things," I told him, "like souvenirs."

That night as I got ready for bed, I stood almost naked while my brother watched a game show on TV, but suddenly I felt his eyes upon me. I turned to him sharply, covering my growing breasts, my sparse pubic hair with my nightgown.

"What are you looking at?" I shouted at him.

"Nothing," he said, looking back at the TV. "Just you."

The next day was the same as before. Same interstate, same oasis, same highway food. We did stop for breakfast at a trucker's stop to vary the pace and ate from a buffet of mashed potatoes, scrambled eggs, pork patties, and grits. Sam and I stuffed ourselves, piling our plates high under my father's disapproving eye, then we sat miserably in the backseat, wishing we'd never eaten at all. At one point Sam spoke despondently, "When's it going to change? When're we going to get there."

"Oh, just wait until the warm breeze blows," my mother said. "You'll see."

As we drove and thoughts of Florida entered her head, I watched my mother let her hand drop along my father's shoulder and she ruffled his hair. He smiled and shook his head and it seemed to me he was shaking her away. "Well," she said, "we'll be there soon."

"Are you watching the maps?" my father said. "Keep the

right maps.'' My mother kept the maps open on her lap, not that we ever needed them because mostly it was a straight drive all the way, but my father wanted the maps ready, just in case.

He was an executive for J. C. Penney and worked downtown in Chicago's Loop. He had helped build the company from the ground up, but he'd had dreams of doing other things. A pilot, a surgeon, a professional golfer. There were the things he claimed he should have done with his life, if he'd been able to do it again. But these dreams all seemed silly to me for he was a man who didn't really like travel or the sight of blood and whose golf game would never improve, not in all the years he lived with us.

Sometimes my mother sewed. She made little needlepoints of butterflies or birds that she'd make into glasses cases to give to her friends. Once in a while they'd talk, though I can't remember much of what was said. Often it was gossip, little things about people they knew. Sometimes it was about the trip. How they hoped the Ponce de León hadn't changed. How they were looking forward to corned beef sandwiches at Wolfies. Sometimes they talked to us. Usually it was to tell us to do or not to do something.

Sam and I sat in the back and at each convenience store, while Sam stood guard, I stole. Key chains, pencils with mementos on their heads, little plastic toys—trees, oranges, birds. Sometimes I took candy or gum, but mainly I took things that wouldn't perish, things that would keep.

———

On the third day the weather changed and we got our first glimpse of the sea. It was off in the distance, some miles from the interstate, but its promise was there, vibrant, blue, lapping the shore. When we crossed into Florida and stopped at the oasis, we bought our first oranges. Sam and I cut ours open, sucking the pulp. My father peeled his carefully, tugging off the skin, then splaying the orange in neat sections like a rose. He handed a slice resting on a paper napkin to my mother, then had one for himself. "This is how you eat an orange," he said, munching on a little section while Sam and I sucked greedily at the pulp. Here I procured my first paperweight—a beach scene with bathers, palmettos inside. When you shook it, a shark came out of the water.

We drove along the coast now on I-95 until we were almost at Miami Beach, the causeway in sight. My mother fumbled with her maps, but this time my father waved her away. "I know how to get there from here," he said. In the end we got lost and drove all the way to Key Biscayne, the beach eluding us as we circled around and around.

The Ponce de León Hotel was on the west side of Collins Avenue, known as the Miracle Mile, but I was surprised it wasn't on the ocean side. I was also surprised at the traffic, the shops. I had expected hanging vines, rosy-billed birds. Our rooms faced the business district, not the ocean side. My mother, sensing our disappointment, suggested we change rooms. We wanted at least to smell the salt air.

"Dear," my mother said gently, "the children want to change rooms. They want to face the ocean."

"What for?" my father said. "They're never going to be in their rooms. They'll be outside all day. And those rooms along the Strip are noisy. I think we're better here."

"Oh, Dad, come on," Sam said. "Who wants to look at a bunch of stores?"

In the end he relented, but reluctantly, for those rooms cost more and he was right in fact about the noise. We could hear the sound of traffic all through the night.

As soon as we were settled in our rooms, Sam and I put on our bathing suits. With our parents trailing behind, we ran across the street, racing to the shore. Then we dove into the ocean without looking back or thinking, our parents in hot pursuit, and for the first time I tasted salt water on my lips. I plunged and rose from the waves while my father, in slippers and socks, shouted to us from the shore.

"Come on in, Dad," I yelled, hoping he would, "the water's fine." My father was afraid of the ocean. He had always been afraid but more so since a few years ago when he was attacked by a Portuguese man-of-war. He was attacked because my mother told him he was the only man she knew who went to Florida every year but would never put his foot into the sea. So one day he did. He went in up to his knees and a Portuguese man-of-war wrapped itself around my father's legs. Then he fell down and the jellyfish wrapped its tentacles around my father's chest.

Now my father wore shoes and socks on the beach because he

was afraid of the men-of-war and he wouldn't set foot near the sea. Instead, as I swam, I could hear him shouting: "Don't you see the flags? Be careful of the current. Don't go out too far."

I thought I'd swim away as I saw him following us along the shore, while my mother buried herself beneath a beach umbrella, zinc oxide on her nose, a crossword on her lap. No matter what we did during those two weeks away, it seemed my mother always sat. She'd find a place and plant herself there. At the pool or the driving range, she'd find her place in the shade, nodding complacently as my father said over and over to himself, "Bend your knees. Keep your head down. Follow through."

So I decided to swim away from them. Not out to sea, but along the shore. I swam as hard as I could, but all along I saw my father racing beside me, like a donkey pulling a barge.

When I got out of the water, breathless and exhilarated, my father rushed to me. "Just what was that all about, young lady?"

"It felt great," I said, shaking my hair.

"Yeah, well, it won't feel so great when a shark takes a bite out of your toes."

That night when I got into bed, after Sam was asleep, I took out the scarf where I kept my souvenirs. I had added a plastic flamingo nightlight, pencils in the shape of coconut palms, shells with stupid faces painted inside. From the light of the street outside, I turned these objects over and over in my hand. I wanted my collection to grow. Sometimes I slept clutching them in my hand.

W e had been promised swamps, alligators, and Indians, and after several days on the beach and pleading by my mother, an outing was planned. We were to take a boat into the Everglades, where we'd see the aquatic birds of my parents' postcards and were told an Indian would wrestle an alligator. I had envisioned a private boat, just the four of us, sailing through the canal of a swamp, manatees eating out of our hand.

When we arrived at the dock, people were already lined up, but my father had purchased our tickets for the outing in advance. He had a small bag with him that contained a camera, mosquito repellent, candy bars. We took our seats near the back of the boat, the four of us lined up as if in a pew while a man with a bullhorn preached, revealing all we were going to see.

It was hot and humid as we sailed through the canal, past birds who stood still as props, though they were the rosy, long-legged kind. Pelicans dove at the sides of the boat. We passed into swamps with dangling vines as the man with the bullhorn, a red bandana around his head, shouted at us the various sights. My father snapped pictures of the motionless birds. My mother took out a handkerchief and kept wiping her brow. I was hot as well, but I kept my eyes on the water, watching for elusive fish.

Then we came to an island with thatched huts. Lethargic Indians with bare chests, black hair cropped square around their heads, helped us off. In a pit alligators dozed, mouths open, teeth bared. One of the Indians prodded an alligator, who seemed annoyed at being aroused, into a sandy ring and it moved obediently to its spot. Then the Indian went in with a stick, and while the alligator snapped one or two perfunctory snaps, the Indian flipped it onto its back, then rubbed its stomach as the alligator went to sleep.

Then the tourists ate sandwiches while the Indian poked the alligator, who flipped over and walked back into its pit. We each gave the Indian a dollar for his work. As we peered into the Indians' thatched huts, where I was sure they did not live, I asked my mother, "Is this what you do? Is this where you go when you used to come alone?"

"Why, of course, dear."

My father overheard me, "Where d'you think we'd go?" Then he snapped at me. "Nothing ever satisfies you, does it? You never appreciate anything. Nothing we do is ever right." Then he turned his eyes back toward the swamp.

There wasn't much to steal there, but I did take some postcards of an Indian wrestling an alligator to the ground, but in the postcards the alligator seemed very fierce, its mouth opened in rage.

That night we went to the Fontainebleau, where my parents bought drinks at the bar——coconut-flavored drinks they drank out of a pineapple with a straw and a little oriental umbrella peeking from the side. My mother's umbrella was pink and my father's green. We got cocktails called a Shirley Temple and a Davy Crockett and our parents gave us the little umbrellas as if we were still small children. My parents drank and laughed. Then some people they'd met one day on the beach came over and sat with them.

Their names were Herb and Iris Miller and they lived in Toledo. Herb Miller was in the shopping center business, so they had a good deal to talk about. And the Millers had adolescent children, so they talked about this as well. They talked about how difficult it was to have children, even as we sat right there, as if we were invisible and couldn't hear a thing.

Herb and Iris's boys suddenly appeared. Their names were Pete and Scott. Pete was fourteen and Scott was my brother's age, and all our parents seemed relieved that we now had friends. When the band struck up, my father asked my mother to dance beneath the bending palms, under the muted lights, and they waltzed, my mother resting her head on my father's arm as she gazed into space, an ocean breeze blowing through their hair.

While our parents danced and drank, I drifted off with Pete. He was in his first year of high school and his parents had been bringing them down to Florida for years. We bought Cokes at the bar and headed to the beach. I waved good-bye to Sam, and Pete gave a little salute to Scott. We walked along the shore where the moon was bright and suddenly Pete flung me to the sand and threw himself over me, just like I'd imagined from the movies. He kissed me, my head pressed against the sand, sending sand into my socks, my underwear, my shirt. He kissed me until he seemed desperate and finally I pulled away. "I'd better get back," I said. "My parents are going to wonder where I am."

But when we returned, our parents were still dancing, just as they had been before, except that now my father was dancing with Iris and my mother was in Herb's arms. My father seemed to dance with Iris exactly as he had with my mother, as if it didn't really matter who was in his arms, and my mother danced with Herb much as she had with my father, that same distant look in her eyes. Then they switched partners again and my parents were back together once more. My mother gazed past his shoulder as if she were looking for something in the night, and my father held her high across her back just as he'd held Iris, his eyes half-closed.

"Come on," Pete said, "let's go back to the beach." I didn't want to, but there was no reason to stay here. "They'll never notice," Pete said, "they won't even know we're gone."

The moon was high, but this time Sam and Scott followed us, though Pete kept shooing his brother away. "Can't you get rid of him?" Pete said.

"Get lost," I said to Sam. "I want to be alone."

Sam stopped in his tracks, then let me go. We walked back down the beach, where once more Pete flung me down, but this time my eyes stayed open, staring at the moon, as if it were happening to someone else.

After a while I got up and left. When I was walking down the corridor to our room, I ran into my father. My hair was disheveled, my clothes a mess. I held my shoes in my hand. "So," he said, "did you have a good time?"

"Yes," I said, "I did."

"Well, that's good." He yawned. "So, see you in the morning."

"Dad," I said, "I'm not tired. Would you like to take a walk?"

"At this hour? I'm beat." He did look tired, his eyes bloodshot. "Tomorrow, okay?" He ruffled my hair.

When I walked into our room, Sam didn't say a thing. He didn't say anything when I went into the bathroom to undress either, though when I emerged, I thought he looked a little sad. Then he went into the bathroom, came out and stared at me, already in bed. I pulled up the sheet, covering my nightgown. "Who the hell brought in all that sand?" was all he said.

On the last day of our trip my father played golf with Herb, my mother had lunch with Iris, and I went into a small shop on the Strip, where I stole again. I stole a dead baby alligator embossed in plastic. It was a tiny, pathetic little thing. I tried to get the shopkeeper to notice me.

I made a lot of noise. I fondled paperweights of flamingos rising in flight, beach scenes, which I let down with a thud, I even dropped pencils, but the shopkeeper, who must have been deaf, hardly looked up. As I stole it, I thought about what it would be like to get caught. Even as I snuck out the door, letting it clang, its bell ringing wildly, he didn't look up. I kept thinking someone would run after me, someone would see.

For years I kept all the souvenirs in the scarf in my closet and I'd take them out from time to time. I even added what I picked up here and there. Nothing that ever mattered much. Things nobody would miss. I'd take them out, listening for sounds in the house that would come, sounds that would make me think I'd better hurry and put these things away.

But it was always silent. No one rushed in. No screams. No shouts. It always seemed to be quiet when I took out my souvenirs. I'd lay them on the bed. The thoroughbred horse, the paperweight beach scene, the embossed baby alligator. There is not much I recall from that trip to Florida. It is all becoming rather a blur in my mind. Most of what I remember is what I stole.

THE
Snowmaker's Wife

Emily woke at daybreak to the sound of Paul's pickup, pulling into the driveway. She always heard him come in, no matter what time she'd gone to bed, no matter what kind of a night she'd had. Some nights she hardly slept. On those she gazed out the window. If there was a moon, she could see the mountain. The mountain was a startling blue in the moonlight and she loved to look at it when she couldn't sleep. Magic Mountain, it was called, a name that had once made her laugh, as if she were living at the foot of a sanatorium and not a famous ski slope.

When Emily looked at the mountain, she thought about Paul. She imagined she could see his tiny form as he checked the trails, measured the snow. He scanned for rough spots, the slick places where ice built up. Sometimes even though Emily could not see him, she could see the whorls he made as he moved up the mountain. Snow devils, they called them. Paul took care of the mountain. He waded in snow waist-deep at night. He worked twelve hours and when he came home he told her what it was like to be alone where no one was. What it was like to be alone with just the sound of the wind.

She heard him shift down and turn off the truck. Then she listened as he clumped the snow off his boots—that thumping sound he made just before he walked in. It used to comfort her—the sound of a man coming home. If they were to see one another during the winter season, it was in this hour when her sleep ended and his began. But now it disturbed her.

The door to their bedroom opened and a cold breeze blew in. Emily snuggled under the covers. With her eyes shut, like a blind person, she read every sound. The boots coming off. The shirt being unbuttoned and draped over the chair. Teeth being brushed; water splashed on his face. Then he sighed, always that sigh, as if something had taken his breath away. Then the covers came back, letting in a chill, as he eased his body in beside hers. She shuddered as his arms reached around her. "It's me," he said as if it could be someone else, "I'm home."

————————

After they made love, Emily sat at the edge of the bed in her nightshirt, shivering. Beside her, Paul slept, his breathing growing deeper. The sky was turning crimson and she had a clear view of the mountain. It was pristine. Nothing on it moved though Paul said that he saw things move. Elk and deer. A few times he came home saying he'd spotted a bear. Last week he claimed to have seen a wolf, though no wolf had been sighted in the White Mountains in decades.

Men alone on the mountains see things from time to time, but no one considers these sightings reliable. But Paul came home and said he'd seen a wolf. His face looked odd, slightly perverse as he told her—an ecstatic look on his face. He described silvery eyes fixed upon him, the dusty gray coat. He said the wolf had stared at him, but when he clapped his hands, it had vanished into the woods. "Maybe it was a dog," Emily said. But Paul said no dog looks like that.

The story of the wolf had made Emily wonder. Perhaps he was just exaggerating, though it wasn't like Paul to exaggerate. He'd always seemed direct, honest. It was one of the things she liked about him. Maybe for some reason he was trying to impress her. Perhaps he sensed she was growing bored with her life. Or he wanted her to think he was in danger when he wasn't. But if he was making this up, what else was he inventing? Other winters he had spent only three nights a week on the mountain, but this season he was spending four, five. Was he really spending them there? She stared at the mountain, white, smooth, and rounded. She had never wondered about this before. But now she did.

The roads were icy as Emily made her way around the hairpin turns. Her wheels slid as she struggled to stay in her lane. Just an hour before, she had eased her way out of bed, unwrapped Paul's limbs from hers where they always fell after making love. She was amazed at how cold his touch felt after a night outdoors, his skin freezing as if he were—frozen solid. Emily didn't do well on slippery roads.

She preferred living here in summer when she'd sit on the porch. In winter she felt old, like a hibernating animal. But in summer she'd sit outside after work and sip Diet Cokes. She'd hike in the woods or work out with Julie. Julie was her friend who worked with her at school. Julie taught physical education, which used to be called gym, and Emily taught language arts— remedial English, composition, writing skills, grammar. She was the only language teacher for the lower grades at the Long Trail grammar school in West Sudbury.

As she drove, Emily thought about the first time she and Paul had seen the house where they'd lived for the past five years. It had been in summer at dusk. They'd driven up and for a moment she'd thought the stars had come to earth. It was fireflies. A million fireflies that illumined the valley. Emily said to Paul, "This is where I want to live." She'd never seen the fireflies again. Then winter settled in and the cold had stunned her. "I had no idea," she said to Paul one morning. "How can you stand it?'' He just shrugged. He loved it, he told her. It was his life.

As Emily drove into town, people stopped to wave. Often they were strangers she hardly knew, certainly not by name. She was late for school but she waved back, smiling like a politician. On holidays baskets of food, baked goods appeared at her door. She received cards from the owner of the general store, a man she'd never met. It was after all "the season."

The seasons here made no sense to her. No one said summer, fall, winter, spring. They said foliage, mud, avalanche, and "the season," the way New Yorkers said "the city." As if everyone should know. Foliage wasn't bad, but "the season" was when the tourists came. In summer everyone, except Emily, got depressed. They didn't know how they'd make ends meet. Restaurants had to live on what they made during "the season." Grocery stores, video rentals barely got by. It was snow they wanted and lots of it. The locals almost all worked in the ski business and its support industries, servicing the tourists. Snow was essential to their lives and to them Paul was a kind of local hero, the man who made the snow.

As she took a turn, smiling at this thought, her wheels spun. Her tires lost their traction as she went into a spin. Turn into the direction of your skid, Paul had told her, but it always seemed wrong. Her impulse was to pull away from the direction she was slipping. She turned the wheel and somehow the car straightened itself out. She found herself on the wrong side of the road, facing the mountain. A shopkeeper rushed to make certain she was all right. A hand went up to stop traffic. Other faces peered at her, nodding, wanting to be sure that she could drive on to her job. She gave them all a thumb's up and they smiled. After all, she was a kind of celebrity too, important in her own way. She was the snowmaker's wife.

Julie was settled into the teachers' lounge, a cup of coffee in her hand, when Emily walked in. Her legs folded under her in her black leotard and skirt, Julie sat nestled like a cat. Sweat was on her brow. She had just taught a gymnastics class. "You're late," she said, tossing back her head of ash blond hair. "Anything wrong?"

"The roads are slick," Emily said. "God, I hate this place in winter."

"Season's what makes this place," Julie said.

Emily just shook her head. She watched Julie pour cream and sugar into her coffee, stirring it with a stick. "How can you drink that stuff?" Emily said. She wondered how Julie kept her figure. She ate French fries and hamburgers without flinching. She never bothered with frozen yogurt, but made her way straight to the Ben & Jerry's chocolate chunks. She did nothing to contain herself. Yet she was willowy.

"It's the way I like it," Julie said. "Besides, I burn it all up." Julie was hot to the touch. Emily had noticed that once when they'd hugged on a cold night. Her skin had burned as if she had a fever. "Are you all right?" Julie asked. "You don't look well."

"I just went into a skid." Emily looked at Julie as she put her books away, her coat in her locker, and settled down with her coffee. She had a few minutes before her first class. "It's a difficult winter. Paul's on the mountain so much."

Julie shrugged. "At least he's somewhere." Julie swore that if she got jilted by one more ski instructor (a Frenchman named René had brought her to Magic in the first place), she'd move to the Caribbean. Where you'll get jilted by scuba instructors, Emily had said.

"It just seems harder this year."

Julie leaned towards her and Emily could see her sharp features. A crease ran across her forehead that Emily had not noticed before. She wondered how Julie survived up here alone. "It's like this every winter, Emily, don't you remember? It's life on the mountain."

"No," Emily said, trying to recall because this year seemed different. "I don't."

As she drove home after work, Emily knew that she was afraid of the mountain. She couldn't explain it. It had come upon her gradually, but she was afraid. It was a sprawling, misshapen mountain, like the body of a person collapsed by the side of the road. From their house on days when she didn't teach she watched the skiers. Then the mountain appeared to her like a toy, a board game, the way the skiers zipped down, the way they fell, picked themselves up, and went on.

Once Emily had gotten lost. She had been skiing when a blizzard began and she couldn't see her hand in front of her face. The slope became impassable. She began to make her way down on the side paths, but soon she found herself on trails that were unfamiliar, service roads Paul used. It was dark and still snowing when she'd reached base lodge and Paul had rushed to meet her. "I can't feel anything below my ankles," she'd said. Inside he'd packed her feet in ice and the pain was unreal, as if needles were being driven into her flesh. In her mind freezing would always be preferable to thawing.

Every year there were accidents, though fortunately not many. Paul took the accidents personally, as if they were his fault. If the slopes were properly covered, if every jagged rock and root were coated in white snow, nothing should happen. Still no one could be blamed when a girl ran into a tree, cracking her spine in two. Or the older man who sailed over the mogul, his skull shattering against a rock off the trail. But mostly there were the ordinary injuries—legs twisted in odd ways, arms dangling limp at someone's side. Avalanches were few and no one had been killed in one in years, but there were warnings every spring at the time when the mountain could break up.

Emily's fear had grown slowly, starting as a healthy respect, but it was more than that now. When she skied, it was on the slopes far below her ability. Paul teased her about this. "I take care of the mountain," he told her. "I know where you can go." But still Emily was afraid.

She knew the rumors, the legends. One was about the Indian woman from the tribe that had once inhabited the White Mountains. She had been shunned by her lover when he had taken another woman as his wife who brought riches and position to his father's family. It was merely a marriage of convenience and though he continued to see the woman he loved, she could not stand the betrayal.

She lured him into a cave and killed him with poison she had brought for him to drink. Then she mauled his body with a bear claw to make it look as if a wild thing had done this. But she could not live with what she had done so she disappeared onto the mountain. A blizzard came and no one ever saw her again, though men lost are said to have been led to safety by a beckoning figure. Others about to freeze to death but later rescued claim that the wind around them seemed to be crying. Still others have been led to their doom. The missing of the mountain, they were called, such as those two boys who thought they saw someone waving and wandered off, never to be found, not even during the spring melt. Or that couple on their honeymoon who were buried alive, their bodies never recovered.

Though Emily did not believe the story Paul told of the wolf, she did believe about the Indian woman. She had woken during a snowstorm and thought she heard crying. Once she was certain the woman was not far from where she stood, perhaps right outside her window. Emily thought she heard tapping on the glass. She wanted to reach out and touch her.

———

aul was getting ready to go to work as she pulled in. She could see him in the light of the kitchen, stirring the pot of soup she'd left on the stove. Often she missed him if she stopped to run errands or pick up some food. But tonight he was there. He kissed her on the nose. "You're cold," he said.

Emily almost never saw Paul doing the things that women see their husbands doing. Coming wet out of the shower, towel wrapped around his waist. Shaving or fixing the leaky faucet. These things he did after he'd woken from his day's sleep before she got home. Mostly what she saw him doing, if she saw him doing anything at all, was sleeping. Once at a zoo they'd visited the habitat of nocturnal animals—bats, raccoons, owls. Emily had been amazed by their activity in the dark. "Just like you," she'd teased.

She gave him a hug. His salt and pepper hair was combed and he was freshly shaved. He smelled of talc and cologne. "You smell good. You need cologne to make snow?" Her voice was not quite a tease.

"You never know who you might run into." He teased her back.

In the corner she saw a pile of his things. "What's that?" she asked. There was an old red sweater he'd worn around the house for years. A pair of comfortable boots.

"Spring cleaning," he said. "Tossing out the old. Bringing in the new."

"It's still winter."

He cupped his hand around her face. "I never get to see your freckles," he said.

"I didn't think you liked my freckles."

He kissed her again. "Why would you say that?" Though he was only in his mid-thirties, she noticed that he was getting that weathered, aging look that comes with life on the mountain.

She looked at the red sweater, the old boots, things he had once been so comfortable in. "You loved that sweater," she said.

"The elbow's torn," he said, pulling on his snow boots. What Paul wanted, Emily knew, was everything perfect. It was what made him love the mountain. Its unspoiled face at night when he was finished with it. He hesitated to leave even his own tracks. He wanted the house just so as well. The way he cooked, the way he cared for his things.

But Emily wasn't perfect. She never knew where to file papers. She let things pile up. She held on to sweaters, socks because she felt cozy in them, never mind the rips and tears. Emily looked at herself in the mirror. Creases were forming in the corners of her eyes as well. She could grab at the soft parts of her flesh. Paul hardly ever saw her in this light. Like the mountain, he saw her in the dark.

She stared at his back. Suddenly she didn't want him to leave. "Why don't you phone in sick. Stay home tonight with me?" she asked, serious now.

He cocked his head. "I have to work. You know I can't do that."

"Oh, you could, if you really wanted to." She wondered how long he'd stay in this business. She thought of the children they were planning to have. Would they start skiing at an early age? She and Paul had been trying for a while. She thought they were having trouble because they made love in the morning and then she had to get up and go to work. She'd been told that to make a baby you have to make love at night and then go to sleep.

He put on his parka and gloves, about to head out into the dark. "Look for me," he said, pointing outside. "I'll be up there."

Later that night she looked for the beams of the snowmobile as it made its way up the mountain. Like a prehistoric beast, a dragon, spewing fire as it went. But tonight the mountain was dark. She kept thinking she'd see the light, the snow devils, the whorl. But she saw nothing at all.

E mily drove to base lodge to have lunch with Julie. On weekends Julie managed the pro shop. This had been her first job when she moved up to Magic with René. Emily had found him handsome, but dull and at the same time self-important. A terrible combination. After that Julie had gotten involved with a bodybuilder who had a huge neck. Emily questioned Julie's taste in men. But as Julie said, "pickings were slim."

Julie was behind the counter. Though they saw one another every day at school, it seemed to Emily that in this harsher light Julie looked tired. But still she had those trim hips and legs, not an ounce of flab on her, and her beautiful golden brown hair.

Her body was a climber's body, and Emily always felt, when she admitted this to herself, that she envied Julie her looks. Not that she approved of this envy. It was just something she couldn't quite help. Emily was smaller, wider, and her brown eyes and hair which people had always called chocolate suddenly seemed ordinary. Julie ate a cheeseburger which dripped from the side of her mouth and a plate of French fries at the Swiss Chalet. Emily had a chef's salad, but wished she were eating red meat and fries. "I'm thinking," Emily said, "of asking Paul to go somewhere else. We've been here too long."

Julie put her sandwich down. "Emily, this winter has been hard on you? What is it?"

"Paul says he saw a wolf on the mountain," Emily said softly.

"Oh, Paul says lots of things." Julie laughed.

"I just think we should go elsewhere."

"Where? Paul's got the best job in the business. Where would he go? Vail? Tahoe? He likes it here."

Emily leaned forward, anger rising in her voice. "What about me? I'm not that happy. He's talked about going into resort management. He could start to think about it now."

"I wish I had a recording. This happens to you every year. You know Paul won't change now." Julie shook her head. "Anyway, it's just the season that's getting you down."

Julie reached for her coffee. It was white, Emily thought, as snow.

———

Emily watched Paul sleeping. He was so peaceful, curled, a slight smile on his lips, hugging the pillow like a little boy. It was rare that she was home during the day and it was odd to watch the sleeper sleeping. She wondered what she was missing by not being able to sleep beside him. Her mother had slept next to her father every night for the ten years of their marriage. After he died, she said she'd never slept quite right again. There was too much room, she said, and she was always cold.

Paul seemed happy when he slept, the way she thought children must. She did not sleep like that. She tossed and turned, the bedding twisting around her. In the morning she had to untangle herself. When Paul slept alone, he could just slip out of bed. It was as if no one had been there at all.

It was snowing and as the day wore on, the snow grew heavier, coming in large, white clumps. It wasn't even like real snow. It did not stop and Emily sat by the window, reading, but not really reading. She watched Paul and she watched the mountain. She stopped to do a few chores, a load of wash, some dishes, but mostly she watched. A foot or more must have fallen. By late afternoon Emily couldn't see the mountain. It had blended in to all the other whiteness. It was as if it weren't there. This made her feel more relaxed.

When he woke, she'd talk to him. She'd say, "It's snowed all day. Do you have to go to the mountain?" Why would he have to go if so much snow had fallen? But she knew the answer. Man-made snow was better than the kind that fell from the sky. Natural snow blew away. It fell off the mountain, leaving rocks exposed, jagged objects sticking out. By morning it would be gone. But you could make the man-made snow any way you wanted. You could make a light powder or heavy packing. You could make popcorn or a soft blanket to line the trails where people tended to slide off. The ground was never smooth. It was the snowmaker's job to cover whatever lay beneath. Everything rough had to be concealed. Sometimes she thought about all the people who worked at night. Why did they call it the graveyard shift? Because that was when the men went to work in the graveyards. Or it was the time when the spirits—and the demons—rose. She wondered about other people who got up at dusk and went out in the cold winds of winter—the night watchmen, the editors who put newspapers to bed, the bakers whose day started before dawn, the continuous processing plant workers. What did families do whose husbands or mothers worked the graveyard shift? Did they see one another much? Did they care?

The snow kept falling and when Paul began to stir, Emily walked over to the bed, sitting down beside him. How could he go to work with all that snow on the mountain? Could he even get to work? Now he turned, stretching like a cat. He reached his arms over his head, then across for her. "How long have you been here?" his voice groggy.

"All day," she replied. "I've been watching you sleep."

"All day?" he asked. "What do you mean?"

She shrugged. "It's been snowing since I got back from lunch." She curled against his chest. "More than a foot has fallen." He patted her head and kissed her.

"Don't go," she whispered. "Stay with me."

He pulled away. "Emily, we've been over this a thousand times. This is what I do. You knew that when you married me. Maybe you could get a job at night."

"As a cocktail waitress?" Emily asked.

Paul shrugged. "I don't know."

"You could go into management."

"I could, but I'm happy outside at night. On the mountain."

"Happier than here with me."

He sighed. "It's like this in winter. You always forget." He got out of bed and put on a pot of coffee. He put some soup on the stove as well and took out a loaf of bread for his supper.

"If you didn't go this once," she asked, following him, "would it make that big a difference? Would it be such a problem just this one time?"

"Someone could get hurt," he said.

"Yes," she replied, "someone could."

When she was not working, Emily drove. She drove into town to buy things she didn't need for meals she wouldn't cook. She drove around the mountain. She paused at vistas, studied views. Everything was so white and the whiteness hurt her eyes.

One day she drove to the gym where Julie was working out. She went up to her friend who was sweating at the stationary bike and said, "I'm sorry to bother you, but I have to talk."

Julie paused in front of Emily in her workout suit of turquoise Spandex, her honey-colored hair tumbling down her shoulders. Julie said she'd get dressed and meet her at Mulligan's in half an hour.

They sat beside the fire and ordered Irish coffees. "You must think I'm crazy," Emily said. She didn't know where to begin. "I have to ask you something, but please don't tell anyone. Do you promise?" Julie promised. "I need to know," she said. "I need to know where Paul is going on the nights when he says he's working."

Julie opened her eyes wide. "Emily, he doesn't go anywhere." She reached across to hold Emily's hand. "He's on the mountain or he's at the office. He's crazy about you. You're all he ever talks about."

"When do you talk to him?"

"Whenever I run into him," Julie sputtered. "Sometimes I see him coming to work on the weekends. It's always Emily this, Emily that."

Emily nodded, watching Julie as she spoke. "Is he seeing another woman?" Emily asked. "I'm sorry to ask you this, but we've been friends for a long time and I've got to know."

"You're alone too much," Julie said. "I know how that can be. I've been alone a bit too much myself lately. Why don't we go out? Go to a movie next week?"

Emily agreed, wondering what was the matter with her.

"You're right," she said. "I do need to get out more."

———

That night it snowed again. A thick blanket fell in the blue light of the moon. Emily had a dream that woke her. The patter of feet dancing through the house. Snowballs hitting the windows. Children beckoning her to follow them into the woods where no trails went. She chased after them, her legs going deeper and deeper into the snow, following red mittens waving until they disappeared over a ridge.

When she woke, she looked outside. It was pure white, the kind of white that frightened her, with no sign of snow devils or the light of the snowmobile. She put on her parka and her boots and got into the car and drove. Her car skidded as she made her way down the hill and she almost went into the ditch. But she pulled out and kept driving. She drove until she came to the road that led up the mountain. She could barely see it through the snow. It was so thick, coming down in big flakes. Could Paul really be up there now? Freezing? Making his way down? When she found him, she'd tell him that she could not go on.

As she wended her way up the mountain road, she saw lights, a brightly lit building by the side of the road. It was the Lift, the tavern at base lodge that stayed open until very late. Paul's pickup was parked in front. Emily pulled up and got out. She stood in the doorway of the warm bar, lit with Christmas lights. It took a moment for her eyes to adjust to the light.

The snowmakers—Paul and his crew—sat at a round table, nursing beers. Froth was on their mustaches and they were laughing about something on the overhead TV. Julie was sitting with them in a green ski suit, though the mountain had been closed for hours. Julie saw her and waved, but Emily just stood there. "Emily," Julie called. "Come join us." She got up to greet her, but Emily turned and walked out into the cold. She heard the sound of feet shuffling. She knew Paul was coming after her. She could hear him calling, racing behind her, but she ran.

There was a trail behind the tavern, heading up to base lodge, and she turned and ran up it. Then she began dodging on to other trails, moving deeper and deeper into the woods. Paul's voice called to her, but soon it drifted away. It was dark on the trail and she hoped no one could see her footprints. At first she ran, but then she stopped. It was so quiet and the air smelled so fresh. She walked into the woods and she saw how nice it was to be alone on the mountain in the dark. She liked the dark suddenly. The sound of only the wind through the trees. She could see why Paul liked it here. She meandered through the woods, her arms brushing against pines that made snow cascade on her head.

For a long time she walked and then she saw the light of the Lift tavern. She had made a circle. When she got back to the tavern, it was closed and all the trucks were gone. Her toes and fingers were cold, but she didn't mind. She got into her car and headed home. As she drove up the driveway she saw that Paul's pickup was already there. He sat with his feet on the dining room table as she walked in. "What was that?" he demanded. "What's the matter with you?" His face was red and she knew he'd been outside for a long time. "I've been looking for you half the night."

"You're seeing Julie," she shouted, "aren't you? You're seeing my friend."

Paul shook his head. "We were on a break. She's dating one of the guys from the crew."

"Don't you think I'd know if she was dating one of the guys? Don't you think she'd tell me?"

He looked shocked. "Emily, I don't know what you're talking about. I don't know what's on your mind."

"You're never here." Tears welled in her eyes. "You're never home."

"I work at night. I come home in the morning. Ask the boys. They'll tell you."

"I'm asking you," she shouted. She was shivering now. Her whole body shaking. "It's freezing in here," she said. She rubbed her arms. "I can't get warm." He pulled her close to the fire and helped her take off her things.

The next day more snow fell and Emily lay in bed, trembling. Paul decided to stay home. He brought her soup and tea. His crew would take care of the mountain. He stayed at her side, but he gazed out the window. Rising at times, he went to the window and tapped, like a moth in a jar. She watched as his eyes scanned the mountain for imperfections, flaws, a mistake he might be able to spot from afar. An accident about to happen.

That night the snow stopped and there was a thaw. A meteorological phenomenon that rarely happened in January. There might be a false spring in February, but not January. The temperature rose to forty, fifty. Paul grew nervous, pacing. He wanted the mountain monitored carefully. He told Emily as she lay feverish that it was as if he could hear it ache, break apart. But he didn't go to work that day or the next. He stayed at her side.

Her fever was high and she was aware of him, hovering beside her, touching her head, then going to the window, just as she had done when she watched him sleep, then returning to her side. He brought her trays with hot drinks. Then she'd hear his voice on the phone. They should lay powder, he told someone. Lots of it. They should look for cracks in the thick deposits along the ridges. They should pack the trails, but not the sides.

But on Monday there was an avalanche. A small one, but still tons of snow had toppled off the southern face. No one was killed, but a member of the ski patrol had a leg crushed as he stood with an entire ski class—twenty teenagers just a few feet away.

Paul was shaken. "Emily," he said, "I don't want to leave you, but there's been an accident, not a serious one, but an accident. I'm going to the mountain. Will you be all right? Can you be here without me?" He touched her forehead. Her fever had broken. She nodded. She would be all right. She felt bad about the accident. She felt bad about everything. Somehow everything seemed to be her fault. "I'm sorry," she said, nestling her face against his hand. "I don't know what came over me."

Paul kissed her on the brow. "I'll be back as soon as I can," he whispered into her ear. "You're alone too much. You need to get out more. We need more time together. I'll call you later."

She wrapped her arms around him. "You're right," she said. "We need more time together. And I should get out more."

"Things will be better," he told her. "I promise. Here," he said, "I made you some coffee."

He handed her a mug of coffee, pale with a swirl of milk. She took it black; she always had. She thought of saying something, but decided against it. "I'll just let it cool," she said, putting the mug by the bedstand. She watched as he pulled on his parka, his boots. He gave her a little wave. Then he was gone.

When he left, it began to turn colder. The light rain that had started to fall was turning to sleet. Ice would cover everything by morning. Ice would glaze the trees, the houses, the fences, the roads. It would be a winter wonderland. Paul would be on the mountain, trying to patch the trails that had turned to ice. Emily drifted in and out of sleep until she heard the crying.

It was coming from right outside the window. She was sure if she opened the window a hand would reach for her. Many nights she had been tempted to open the window when she heard the crying, but she never had. Now she wanted to. It seemed like the right thing to do. She knew that the hand that was waiting for her would be cold.

Around the World

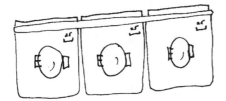

I'd never seen him at the laundromat before. If I had, I would've remembered because Blue Mesa where we live is a small town and not that many newcomers use the laundromat, even though it's a nice place to do your clothes. Lots of big cream-colored machines that go around, bright neon lights overhead. I like this laundromat because it has big wire baskets where you can stick your clothes as you move them from washing machine to dryer and because they've got big tables where you can fold. I love to fold. I love to take hot towels or even Scott's jeans and wrap my arms in them and smell how clean they are and let the warmth rush over me while I fold.

He was blond and taut and stood just outside the door smoking when I came back in after talking to Patti on the phone. Patti is my girlhood friend. I drop my kids off at Patti's or she drops hers off at my place when we've got things to do, but usually once we get somewhere we just call each other on the phone so it seems silly to go any place since we could just sit at the kitchen table and talk at home. From the laundromat phone, that's right beside the gas pump, I talked to Patti for a while about Ross, her husband, who was coming home later and later, and when I got off the phone, the blond man was standing there, smoking.

I probably wouldn't have even noticed him if I hadn't come back and seen that the wash in my dryer wasn't mine. I knew it wasn't mine the minute I looked in and saw. Because I never mix my whites with my colors, not even to dry. I always keep them nice and separate so the dark lint doesn't get on the baby's things or mix in with Scott's shirts. Not that Scott would care. He hardly ever wears a white shirt unless it's a Sunday and maybe we go to church, if he's up in time. But it's a point of pride with me, to do my wash this way.

But that day I looked in and saw how a green sock was floating with white underwear, the Jockey, not the boxer kind, and jeans mixed in with white T-shirts and so I knew that wash was not mine. At first I thought mine had been stolen, which happens sometimes with drifters coming through, but then I saw it piled in one of the wire baskets. Scott's jeans weren't even dry. I picked them up and pressed them to my cheek. They still had that wet feel along the seams that Scott would notice right away if he put them on.

Scott's jeans always took so long to wash. There was all that horse hair and stench. Always a bad smell I couldn't quite get out. But everything seemed to smell that way to me. Sometimes I'd lay in bed at night and just smell the rooms around me. The smell of children, of talc and urine and sweat, the smells of the dogs and cats who wandered in and out of rooms, the smell of clover and wheat, of horse and hay, the sweet, stale smell that got into all Scott's clothes, into his hair, into his nails, that got into my body when he made love to me. And when he lay on top of me, after making love, I could smell the horses as if they were right there in the room.

When I saw that the clothes in the dryer weren't mine and mine were sitting still damp in a wire basket, that was when I looked at him. It was the first I saw him really and he was looking at me and so I said, "Excuse me, but did you take my wash out of the dryer?"

"It had stopped," he said, looking at me with very sharp eyes like a weasel.

"It wasn't dry."

"It was just sitting there," he said, taking a drag.

I fumbled through my things, starting to sort them. I would have put them back in, but all the dryers were full. "I'm missing a red sock," I said, holding up a mateless one. The blond man looked at me dumbly. "I said I'm missing a sock."

"Then you lost it, lady, before I got here."

At first I thought he might be a cowpuncher on the rodeo circuit since they sometimes came in and out of town in the summer when the season was on, but there was something too neat about him, too clean, and he had that look that I'd seen in the eyes of the college kids, a look like he had some place to go and it wasn't here. And then when I walked by him, dragging my basket in a huff, there wasn't any smell to him at all and his hands looked soft so I knew he'd never held a rope and that he was just passing through on his way somewhere else.

He's the kind of guy they have over at the college—clean-cut and trim, everything just right—and I would've thought he was from there, if the college was in session. Then it occurred to me he's too old to be a student. There was something a little knowing about his eyes like someone who's already been out in the world. But he's got that wired look so I decide he's the new track and field coach, the one they were advertising for last year.

I've got my own plans to travel. I have a Maxwell House coffee can in the kitchen where I keep the money I've saved, not much, but enough to get me to San Diego someday, maybe Disneyland. I have this longing to see the sea. I've always been on Mountain Time. I've only heard about this place where the water meets the land or seen the way the surf comes crashing into the shore at the start of *One Life to Live*. I'll be lucky to make it to Montrose or Grand Junction, but I'm saving to get to San Diego and see the sea.

That night Scott comes home and does what he always does. Gives me a kiss on the cheek and a pat on the rear. His mustache tickles my ear and I pull a little bit away. Then he pops a beer and takes the kids out to the corral for a pony ride. I'm left standing at the sink, snipping the stems off the beans, and then I stop.

From the sink I can see out to the corral, out towards the mountains across Blue Mesa. I look out across this place where I've lived my entire life, and I see the mountains and the sky. I see my husband who I've been with since I am fifteen years old, and my three children, going around on the spotted pony. Scott takes a sip from his Coors but he is careful not to let Stephanie fall. Stephanie is the baby, the one who didn't come out right, and we have to watch her all the time. The other two are all right, except Scott Junior doesn't always go to school. And Nicole is going to drive herself crazy, always trying to do everything right. I watch this scene, the same one I see every night, and try to think about what will happen after the children are grown. What will I see from this window?

I close my eyes, trying to imagine, and what I see is the blond man from the laundromat. This surprises me because all my life I've been with Scott and I've never even thought of myself with another man. But suddenly I see this long drink of water, skinny blond guy and our clothes all neat and folded by the side of a bed, sweet smelling, and I think of his soft hands and his doe-skin flesh. I close my eyes and for an instant shut out what I've always known.

When I open them, everyone is there and they want dinner on the table. Stephanie talks as best she can and tries to tell me what she'd like, her body bobbing back and forth as she stammers, and Scott Junior takes a Coke, even though I tell him not to, while Nicole, the only one who really helps me so it's hard to fault her, sets the table, but I can see she's not happy about having pot roast again. Then, just before dinner, Patti calls. She says Ross isn't home yet and she's locking him out. She says that any man who isn't home by seven o'clock doesn't deserve to eat. She's going to put his dinner on the porch and put the bolt across the door. She says, "Do you think my husband is seeing another woman? Do you think there's someone else in his life?"

The rodeo was opening at the fairgrounds Friday night and on Sunday I went to watch the carnival being set up. It's something I like to do each year. I like watching it get set up and taken down. I like thinking about where it's been and where it's going, how it never stays in any place too long.

It always takes them so long to set up, a week maybe or more, and so before the carnival even opens, I've got a week when I go and just watch. Usually I take the girls because what else am I going to do with them. We go and sit in the car and watch the lights being set up or the Ferris wheel get put together. I make them all kinds of promises I can actually keep like that I'll buy them cotton candy or let them jump until they drop on the Kiddie Kastle. Or if Scott Junior comes along I tease him about the last time he went on the Tilt-o-Whirl. But mostly I like to just sit and watch the men as they raise the canvas and the poles, or the bright lights of the Ferris wheel as it begins to spin.

Another thing I love about the carnival is how Scott will watch the kids while I go on every ride. It's almost the only time I'm ever really alone and get to just be with myself. Scott won't go on the big rides because he gets sick, but he'll watch me from the wings as I ride the Sizzlers, the Salt and Pepper Shakers, and the Around the World. I like Around the World best because it doesn't tip you or spin you or make you twirl. It just hurls you out with its arms and you feel as if you can just keep going; how if it released you, nothing would keep you down.

I sit until dusk with the girls in the backseat, as the concessions go up, the lights turning on, all shimmering against the pale pink Colorado sky even though Nicole keeps saying, "Mommy, can't we go home" and I have to shush her. I just sit and stare until finally it gets dark and I have to take everybody home.

Scott and Ross are watching a game, drinking beer, as we walk in. The phone's ringing off the hook. I know it's Patti, ready to skin Ross alive. Any minute her car will swing in the drive and I'll have to stand between the two of them. Suddenly I feel tired and wish I could just go to bed. I think of the carnival lights. How beautiful they are against the sky.

I know a methodical person when I meet one and I think this guy's that way so if he's still in town, he'll be doing his wash on Tuesday. On Tuesday I go back to the laundromat, same time. Patti doesn't want to take the kids but I say it's something

I just have to do. Then I put on a tight pair of jeans and some lipstick and go just at the time I think he'll show up, but he's not there. I start to do my wash, separating the clothes very slowly. I think how noisy this place is with all the machines going around. I'm starting my spin cycle when he arrives, dragging a big brown laundry bag behind him. He speaks to me first. He says, "Did you find your sock?"

"Yes, it was caught up in the legs of a pair of jeans."

"I told you," he says, "I don't leave anything behind."

We do our wash in machines across from one another. I watch as he puts fabric softener in, measuring out just the right amount. Later I see him put a Bounce in his dryer and I'm impressed. I think to myself maybe I don't need to separate my whites and colors in the dryer. Maybe he knows something I don't know. "You're not from around here," I say.

And he smiles and says, "No, I'm sure not. I'm from California." He says it in such a way I can tell he's proud. I think how he's someone who comes from the place where I want to be.

"What's it like there?" I ask.

"Oh, you know, ocean, beach, freeways, same old stuff."

"Yeah," I say, "I know." I'm afraid he'll ask me what I know, so I turn back to the work I have to do.

"And you?"

"I'm from around here."

He's starting to fold. "Seems like a nice place to be from."

"You going to be here long?"

He shakes his head. "I travel for business," he says.

"Rodeo?" I ask. Scott used to do the circuit before Scott Junior was born. He did cattle roping and broncos until one day a horse tossed him twenty feet, then stomped on his ribs. In the hospital I told him he had to stop. I said it was rodeo or me. But the blond man just laughs, shaking his head. "Now, do I look like that kind of a guy?" When he says this, he leans against the folding table in my direction, his elbows resting on his warm T-shirts and towels. His face is only inches from mine. I feel his breath against my face, hot and steamy like the air from the machines.

Even though I promised Patti I'd be back by five, I stop at the carnival on the way home and see that it's mostly up. They've got their lights on and the music is playing. The Ferris wheel is already going around. I stand there until the sky darkens and the lights are bright against the sky. Patti's in a huff when I pick up the kids. She looks me up and down, clicking her tongue inside her mouth. "I've never known you to have that much wash to do."

When I get home, Scott's sitting in front of the baseball game, beer in hand. "The carnival's up," I say. "Maybe we can go later."

"We'll go Friday," Scott says, "I wanta watch the game."

"So, Friday," I say.

Even as I say it, I think of the man from the laundromat. I think how Friday is three days away and he does his wash on Tuesday, and how that means another week until I see him again, but I've got the carnival to look forward to on Friday. I've already made up my mind what I'm going to do when I see him again. I'm going to ask him for his address. I'm going to tell him that I expect to be visiting California soon and I'd like to look him up. I'll tell him how I don't know anyone there and how it would be nice to have someone to call. I think how that won't seem forward or out of place. Maybe he'll give me a business card with his home number scribbled on the back. And I'm sure I can call him at home. But I'll ask politely, "Would your wife mind if I call?" but of course there's no wife because why would he be on the road, doing his laundry on his own.

That night in bed Scott lays beside me and I think how he has been with me for fifteen years, been my husband for the last ten. And I don't know what he thinks about as he lays in bed. I have no idea what's on his mind. I decide to ask him. I say, "Honey, what are you thinking about?" And he replies, "I'm thinking about the cattle I have to move off the mountain next week." What more can I say? After a man says something like that to a woman, what is there to say?

The kids are ready at six sharp on Friday, but Scott hasn't walked in the door. Stephanie is already starting to bawl and bob back and forth and Scott Junior says to hell with it, he isn't going, but then Scott comes in with no time to shower. I say, "Aren't you going to change at least? Aren't you going to wear other clothes," but the kids are all fighting by this time, so we get in the van and leave.

When we get to the carnival, it is all lit up, a bright pink and green and yellow against a purple sky. It is as if a spaceship had landed right in the middle of Blue Mesa where we live. The minute the kids see it, they scream with delight. Stephanie bobs as fast as I've ever seen her and Nicole has to put her hands on her sister to hold her back. Scott Junior is out of the car in a flash, heading for the baseball throw. Nicole takes Stephanie by the hand and Scott puts his arm around me as together we walk among the concessions and rides.

Stephanie wants to go jumping on Kiddie Kastle and Nicole takes her there while Scott and Scott Junior go off to toss some rings and balls. Then I take the girls to the merry-go-round and watch them go around, Stephanie with her head thrust back, laughing all the way, and Nicole, holding on to her, sweet as can be. I stand there, watching them, holding on to one another, and I know how I could never leave them really, but if I could just go away for a little while, just step out of my life into someone else's, I'd be better; I'd be fine.

When Scott comes back, he's won a picture of Elvis in a wooden frame and a giant roadrunner stuffed animal. He scoops Stephanie into his arm and says I could go on some rides and he'll watch the kids. First I do the Tilt-o-Whirl with Scott Junior, but then I want to go on the bigger rides, the ones I know he doesn't like because he is a tough kid with a weak stomach and with him it's all show. He wouldn't set foot on the Sizzler or the Hot Tamale. So I do those rides first.

Then I look at the Around the World. The ride just sits there, like a wilted plant, but I know what will happen when it starts up soon. I pay my ticket and get into my little cab. As the ride starts up its arms begin to extend like the tentacles of an octopus. My cab begins to rise and I see my family on the ground. Scott with the portrait of Elvis in one hand and Stepha-

nie in the other. In his cowboy boots and hat, I can't see his face
and he reminds me of one of those faceless guys they used to
have in the Dick Tracy comics.

The ride starts up, slowly at first, then faster and faster,
gathering speed. I see them beneath me, waving as the ride
spins me away. Soon I am parallel to the ground and can't see
them anymore. All I see is mountains, mere shadows in the
distance, as I rise above the carnival lights and press my head
back, gazing into the night sky. I imagine myself on a mission
hurtling through space. I go around and around and feel as if I
could just keep on going. Then the ride begins to slow down. I
feel it losing momentum, feel myself dropping back to earth. As
it begins to slow, it seems as if my stomach has been left
behind. Slowly my family comes into view and they are waving,
as if I have been away for a long time, and I wave back, as if I
have.

Scott helps me down and Nicole and Stephanie cling to my
arms. I am wobbly as a newborn calf. The night sky is beautiful
and the Milky Way runs overhead as if painted in yellow Day-
Glo. Scott takes me by the arm, seeing I am breathless, and puts
his hand to my forehead. "You're red. Are you all right?"

I feel as if I can breathe again after having my face in a plastic
bag. "I'm fine," I say. "I'm all right." Scott wants to play
darts. He puts his arm around me and says there's a nice concession with velvet paintings, the kind he knows I like to put
over the mantel or hang in the kids' rooms. He promises he'll
win one for me. I think how sweet it is of Scott to think of me,
how he is good for remembering the little things.

As we cross the arcade, Patti and Ross are walking just ahead of us. They've got their arms around one another like sweethearts and the kids are nowhere in sight. He keeps slipping his hand into her back pocket and she keeps taking it out, putting it around her waist. They turn off the side of the arcade onto the darkened fairgrounds. I think how Patti's always complaining to me, how her life is a roller coaster, but I think how maybe she's lucky it's not like mine, flat like the mesa where we live.

We head in the direction of the dart concession. Barkers call. They offer us their giant stuffed animals, their velvet paintings, their Kewpie dolls. "Here," one shouts, "make this basket and make my day." Another throws a softball, "Easy as pie." From the distance I can see the barker at the dart concession where Scott is leading me. He hurls darts backwards over his shoulder, popping balloons behind him, and calling out to passersby.

I recognize him, not by his face, but by his clean pressed look, by the way everything fits so smooth around his skin. At first I don't think he recognizes me, but slowly it seems to come to him and he smiles a crooked smile. "Here," he says, looking Scott up and down, "win one for the lady."

"Let's go," I say, "I don't want any of those," pointing at the velvet paintings. But Scott knows I do because I'm always asking for more paintings to put on the walls and make our house look more like a home.

Scott takes the darts and puts his dollar down. He bites his mustache, takes careful aim. He misses the first, then the second. He puts another dollar down, then misses again. Scott Junior wants to play and Scott puts money down for him. I wish

I hadn't eaten the cotton candy and the popcorn with the kids and I'm wishing I hadn't gone on any of the big rides at all because my stomach is starting to feel shaky, the way Scott Junior's always does.

I think Scott is ready to stop playing, but the blond man keeps saying, "Come on. Win one for the lady." I feel his eyes on me as if he knows something about me I don't even know. Scott tries again. He pulls in his breath and throws the dart with all his force, but the balloon just seems to move out of his way. So now the blond man jumps down.

"Here," he says, "let me help you." He takes the darts and tosses them one, two, three over his head. The balloons all pop. "Take your pick," he says to me. "Which one will it be?" Scott, looking dejected now with the Elvis picture in his hand, doesn't say a word. I think how I've only seen him look this way once before, the time the bronco busted in his ribs.

I look over the prizes. Velvet paintings of mountain streams and wild beasts, Mexican villages and beautiful girls. "No thank you," I say.

But the blond man says take it, so I pick the lions—big yellow lions—from halfway around the world against a blue velvet background to hang above Stephanie's bed. Stephanie bobs beside me, rubbing the velvet with her hand. "Thank you," I say. "Our daughter will like this."

The blond man from the laundromat smiles as if we are partners in a scam. "See you," he says.

As we start to leave, a toothless lady barker beckons to me with tobacco-stained fingers. The children still want to play, but

I look at the prizes—giant stuffed animals that look gray and frayed like they've seen too many carnivals where nobody has won. I clutch the girls by the hands, leading them away, and tell Scott Junior to walk straight ahead. It is late as we get to the car. I turn and look back to see the carnival for the last time, shimmering against the sky, and I think how I can see all the pieces and joints where it is assembled. How it looks as if it could all come tumbling down.

That night when we get home, everything feels dirty and I can't seem to get the odor of the carnival off my skin. The kids' clothes are dusty. Stephanie's pants have a syrupy goo on the leg and Scott Junior's shirt is covered with grime. Even Nicole, who is normally so neat, has gum on her socks. So I think I'll do the wash tomorrow, even though it's Saturday. I'll do it even though the laundromat will be full and it's not my washing day.

Losing Track

They saw the first sign miles back. "Dinosaur tracks," it read. "I want to stop," Melanie said. "I want to see them." Hal didn't protest. The signs were pointing their way.

On their trip they'd seen all the usual things. The dam, the canyon, the valley with its strange eroded shapes. Hal had captured Melanie in photos at the canyon rim at dusk and protesting on the back of a mule at midday. They'd stopped at every scenic view and lookout, read every historic marker, taken pictures at each horizon. Now they were on their way home.

The Winnebago was holding up well. They'd refurbished it for the journey, complete with microwave and miniature dishwasher. "I'm not traveling for two months without a dishwasher," Melanie had said. But since they'd been on the road, she almost wished she hadn't bothered. It wasn't much doing dishes for just the two of them.

The signs were handwritten, almost in a child's scrawl, and Melanie had counted four since she'd seen the first one. "Dinosaur tracks, straight ahead." And then a faint arrow pointing in the direction they were headed. "We won't even have to go out of our way," she told Hal, knowing that was something he hated to do. "We can probably just pull off the road."

They had begun planning the trip almost a year ago, though at first Melanie had resisted. "What if Kelly calls while we're away," she'd said. "What if she decides to come home then?" Kelly, their youngest daughter, had disappeared two years before. But Hal had gone ahead and put the better part of his year's commission into the Winnebago. He was a real estate broker for Century 21. A salesman of parcels of land. He wore the brown and yellow jacket of all Century 21 brokers—a jacket that Melanie said made him look like a wasp—and took hopefuls in and out of other people's homes.

Melanie was a high school teacher of geometry, and they'd never seen the Wild West before. This tour of the national parks was for them a dream they'd talked about for years. It was what they'd wanted to do as soon as the kids were grown. They hadn't minded the traffic jams in Yellowstone or the grizzly warnings posted in Glacier. They hadn't minded the lines of Japanese and German tourists stomping around the Grand Canyon. They both agreed it was the trip of a lifetime.

At Four Corners Hal had, despite Melanie's embarrassment, squatted down on all fours, managing to put his legs in Utah and Colorado, his hands in New Mexico and Arizona, and said he felt like king of the world.

Seeing him spread like that across four states, Melanie had thought how he was the only man she'd known. They'd met at Disneyland on the Pirates of the Caribbean ride when they were fourteen. They'd stood in line behind one another and shared a little boat that carried them wordlessly past the magic lantern and Spanish moss of the Blue Bayou and then hurled them screaming into the dungeons where captives pleaded for mercy. She had clutched his arm. The thrust into darkness had sealed their fate.

T he signs were erratic. Sometimes they were very frequent. Other times they disappeared, and then Melanie despaired of ever following them anywhere. Then they'd come again, only to fade, making Melanie think that they must have passed the place where the dinosaurs had been. Then they'd appear, more insistent than before. "Dinosaur tracks ahead. You must stop here. Don't miss." Melanie didn't know why she wanted to see them. They had already seen so much. Hal had planned their trip down to the last detail, booking each campsite well in advance. He had surprised her with the brief white-water rafting tour down the little tributary of the Colorado and with a night in a cement teepee with "Rent Me" painted on its side. She'd done things on this trip she'd never dreamed of doing before.

But she had never seen real dinosaur tracks. Once as a girl her mother had gotten her a dinosaur diorama, and she tried to imagine what had lived twenty-five million years ago, what had wiped them out. But she hadn't thought of dinosaurs much since then, not until she began seeing the signs. Now she had to see where the signs were leading them.

"I'm not sure," Hal said after a while. "It might take us out of our way."

"Well, worse things could happen," Melanie said.

Hal shook his head, pondering this for a time. It was the way things had been with him—tilting his head and pondering in silence for long periods—ever since Kelly had disappeared. She was alive, lost in America, that was all they knew. They knew she wasn't dead because every few months or so a card would come that read, "I'm fine, Kelly." Those cards were the only things, Melanie thought at times, that kept them from going insane.

Kelly had disappeared with that no-good boyfriend of hers, a biker, when she was just seventeen. Hal had forbidden her to keep seeing him, so one day she got on the back of his Harley at five A.M. in front of their Mission Viejo home and disappeared. Melanie hadn't wanted to make this trip because she'd thought,

What if Kelly returns? What if this is the time she decides to come home and I'm not there? "She'll ask a neighbor, for Christ's sake," Hal had said. But then he'd added more gently, "Besides, it will do you good to get away for a while." In the end Melanie had taped a letter to the door and left a message on the answering machine. "If this is Kelly calling, we'll be home in August. Please tell us where you are. If it's anyone else, leave a message when you hear the beep." Melanie didn't care who heard this message. She didn't care who knew of their private grief.

It had been a long time since they'd seen a sign. "We must've passed it," Hal said.

"No," Melanie replied firmly, "I'm sure we haven't."

"Who cares about these swamp-bound, pea-brained creatures," Hal said with a smile. "I'm interested in the here and now." He tapped the wheel with his fingers. But he decided to humor her. After all, she'd given him the videocam for the trip. She'd even held it as he pretended to be jumping into the Grand Canyon. So since they were on their way home and she wanted to see dinosaur tracks, well, he reasoned, let her see them.

They hadn't noticed how the terrain had changed. But now they drove across a landscape with no buildings in sight except for the occasional farmhouse or roundhouses that Melanie wondered about. The land itself looked prehistoric. The earth turned a deep shade of red. Giant red forms, like sculptures, suddenly appeared on the horizon. Sometimes the road descended into canyons with huge rocks jutting up on either side. But otherwise they were traveling across a flat, red terrain where as far as they could see there was nothing but giant billowy clouds. Thunderstorms formed in the distance; sheets of rain could be seen coming down.

Cars were replaced by pickups, RVs by battered minivans with rusty bodies. The women had long dark hair. The men were dark and wore cowboy hats. She opened the map, trying to figure out where they were or if they had taken a wrong turn. But the AAA TripTik made it clear that this was the way to go. Hal turned on the radio to get some news, but the only station he could reach had a deep chanting voice, singing in rhythmic hums. They were crossing Navajo land.

It was almost two o'clock when they stopped at a restaurant in a small town for lunch. It was the only town and restaurant they had seen for quite a while, and they were hungry, so they decided to stop. They parked and walked into the Red Sands. All the women had black braids. The men all wore a single braided ponytail. One of the men was putting up an American flag with an Indian in the middle. Hal shook his head. Melanie showed him the map where AAA had made a circle in this town, but she saw that Hal didn't like it at all.

Melanie thought the restaurant was nice. It had posters of John Wayne—the Duke, they called him back in Orange County, where she was from—and Marlboro men on the wall. There were ads for Cherokee vans with Indians posing in front of them. A sign read, "Nobody knows the trail better," from the U.S. West Information Centers, with cowboys and Indians galloping across the plains.

In one corner three blond people sat, and Hal and Melanie

went to sit near them, but they were speaking a foreign language, which Melanie decided was German or Dutch. The Navajo station played chants on the loudspeakers and Hal grimaced. "I wish they'd turn that down," he said.

But Melanie said she liked it. "It's a soothing sound," she said, closing her eyes. "I feel like a baby being lulled to sleep."

A man with a white ribbon woven through his braid came to take their order. Hal asked for a beer and the man said, "No beer."

"No beer?"

"No beer on the reservation."

Hal frowned. "How big is this reservation?" he asked.

"You've got two hundred more miles," the Indian said.

Melanie ordered a green-chili omelette with sour cream. "Just to try something different," she said.

Hal ordered a hamburger and fries.

When the Indian returned with their order, Melanie said, "Excuse me, but do you know where the dinosaur tracks are?"

"The dinosaur tracks?" the Indian asked. "You want to see the tracks? Then go to Shonto. You will see the sign."

Melanie flipped through the TripTik, looking for Shonto. The Indian looked at her squarely. He had deep-set eyes, a furrowed brow, and pockmarked skin. "What you are looking for," he said very distinctly, as if he expected her to commit this to memory, "is Head of Mother Earth Mountain."

"Head of Mother Earth," Melanie repeated.

"This is where the dinosaur tracks are, if that is what you want to find."

Melanie looked at him oddly. Hal glanced up from the map. "Shonto. Is it out of our way?"

The Indian looked puzzled. "Is what out of your way?"

"The dinosaur tracks," Hal said.

"I'm not sure what you mean," the Indian said, "but I'm sure it is not out of your way."

Melanie dozed in the RV after lunch as they drove in the direction of Shonto. Hal thought it would be at least a ten-mile detour, and he began to grumble. When he got this way, Melanie willed herself to sleep. As she slept, she didn't dream of Kelly as she often did when she was just dozing. And she didn't dream the dream that had recently come to her many times: that she was holding a baby in her arms—a baby in a diaper who sucked on a bottle—except the baby was a full-grown woman she held and rocked and cooed to. This time she dreamed of beasts, of dinosaurs, giant lumbering creatures roaming the land. She saw them wandering the bubbly terrain. She saw their giant feet come down, leaving a trace. It was the dinosaurs who came to her, and she imagined that from beneath the layers of sediment, creatures rose from the ruins.

When she awoke they were driving on a dirt road, and she had no sense of how long she had been asleep. It could have been moments or days. If Hal hadn't said "Damn" when the road turned to gravel, she was sure she would have just slept on.

"Oh," she said, rubbing her eyes, "it can't be far on this road. Did you see a sign?"

"A sign for what?"

"For the tracks. Have you seen another sign?"

"There was one at the turnoff about a mile back. It said five miles."

"Good."

He reminded her that the last sign had said ten miles, and that was hours ago. "What kind of place is this? Can't get good directions. Can't get a drink."

"I like it," Melanie said. "I don't know why."

One of the things Melanie liked was that she hadn't thought about Kelly in a while. She hadn't, for example, dreamed about Kelly. She hadn't looked at the back of each motorcycle, thinking maybe she'd see her daughter there. She hadn't thought about the last time she saw her, the night before she disappeared. Kelly was sitting up in bed, uncharacteristically still, reading, in a pink nightie, and Melanie, not wanting to disturb her, had just stood in the doorway and blown her a kiss. "I should have gone to her," Melanie has said dozens of times since Kelly has been gone. "I shouldn't have just stood at the door."

She also hadn't thought about what she thinks about most often—Kelly's return. Melanie likes to run this scenario through her mind. How she will be standing in the kitchen when she hears the motorcycle pull up. How she'll stop as if frozen in time as the engine dies in front of her house. Then she'll go to the window and see Kelly walking up the front

walk, her dark curls flying in the wind. When Melanie thinks of
this, she often bursts into tears no matter where she is, no
matter what she is doing. If Hal is with her, he always says the
same thing. "You have two perfectly good children. I don't
know why you are breaking your heart over this one." But
often later she'll find him weeping. "You know," he'll say,
"she is my daughter, too."

When she first disappeared, they tried to find her. They filed
missing-person reports with the police throughout California.
They ran ads in all the major newspapers in the West. They
even hired a detective, but no one came up with any leads.
Finally a police officer said to them, "Do you know how many
kids like yours are missing out there?" his hands sweeping
across the country. The best thing, he told them, is to stay
home and wait.

For almost two years Melanie stayed home. She would hardly
go to the store. If she did, she put the answering machine on,
always stating how long she'd be gone. If she came home and
there was a hang-up, she'd play it over and over, listening for
the slightest sound, a clue to where the caller might have been
calling from. She couldn't answer the door or the phone without a flicker of hope that this time it would be Kelly. And now
for the first time in those years—since they'd begun looking for
the dinosaur tracks—Melanie had hardly thought of her at all.

At the trading post in Shonto they stopped for supplies. Four
or five Indians sat in front of the building. As the RV pulled in
they got up and stared. Not many RVs come to this trading
post, Melanie thought. "How far to the dinosaur tracks?" Hal

asked. "Not far," said the old Indian who worked at the register. "Just up the road."

Melanie smiled an "I told you so" smile. They shopped for Hamburger Helper, bananas, Diet Cokes, and Oreos. An old woman in the corner was selling beads, and Melanie stopped to look. The old woman looked at Melanie for a long time. Then she tied a blue beaded bracelet around Melanie's wrist. "Oh, no," Melanie said, but the old woman motioned for her to keep it. When Melanie reached into her purse for money, the old woman pushed Melanie's purse away. All the Indians at the trading post looked at Melanie intently when the old woman did this.

The road went from bad to worse. It narrowed abruptly and became a single lane. The potholes were enormous and they banged the bottom of the Winnebago. Huge dips were in the road. Hal kept cursing under his breath. Melanie looked outside and saw the landscape. It was mountainous and strange. The hills came in colors—red, green, brown—that made them look as if someone had painted them. Then they saw the last real sign they knew they'd see. "Dinosaur tracks. Straight ahead." Melanie sighed with relief. "Well, I guess there's no going back now."

As they rounded the bend and came to a valley of huge pink and yellow craters that made them think they were on the moon, the Winnebago stalled. A gush of steam rose from the radiator. Hal jumped down, opened the hood, released the radiator valve. Then he leaped back as steam burst like Old

Faithful. "Damn it," he said. The RV had overheated from the heat and the strain.

"We could probably just walk down the road," Melanie suggested. "I'm sure it's not far now. Maybe someone there can help us."

"I'm not leaving this van," Hal said. "It'll cool down, and we'll go ahead."

Unsure of what was best, Melanie put some Hamburger Helper in the skillet with some ground beef she had in the fridge. Hal popped a couple of beers that were left in the cooler. "I think it's kind of romantic," Melanie said, lighting a candle. "Just the two of us here."

"Yeah," he said. "No hookup, no electricity, no water."

It was their first night not in an RV park, Melanie agreed, but it was a beautiful spot. She looked at the mountain straight ahead, behind which a fiery orange sun was setting. A cathedral-like silence fell across the valley. The head of a woman looked down on her, bemused, staring straight at them. "That's it," Melanie said. "That's Head of Mother Earth Mountain."

Hal looked up. "Where?"

"Right there," Melanie said. "See?" With her finger, Melanie traced the outline of the woman's face. "She's looking down on us."

"Well, I'm glad someone is," Hal said as he tried to start the engine, "because we aren't going anywhere tonight."

After they ate the hamburger and drank some beers, thunder cracked. Rain pounded the top of the RV. Hal groaned as they sat in the candlelight. Melanie moved against his arm, curling close. She raised her mouth to his, but he pulled away. "Not here," he said. "I'm too nervous. I want to listen, in case anything comes."

"We're locked inside the RV," she said. "The only thing that could come is help."

"Or some of those Indians from back there."

Melanie put her hand on his. "Maybe you're uncomfortable because we're off the beaten track."

"I'm uncomfortable because things can happen."

"I don't think anything bad will happen to us here." She spoke with authority, as if she knew, but Hal would not be moved. She saw how frightened he was. He was able to do only what they'd planned for. He had never liked surprises, spontaneous events, sudden changes. He ate the same thing for breakfast each morning. He had played golf with the same foursome since he was a young man. He and Melanie had made love on Tuesday night and Sunday morning for years. On trips Hal always kept a map open at his side. He liked to know exactly where he was going and what he was getting.

Kelly used to tease her father about this. She'd say to him when they'd all get into the van and go on a car trip, "So what if we lose our way for a while? So what if we don't have a place to stay for one night?" Or she'd say, "Come on, Dad, live dangerously. Eat in a restaurant you haven't been to before."

Kelly always liked doing things spur-of-the-moment. A friend would call and she'd be out the door. If a boy wanted to ask her out for the weekend, she'd tell him to call her on Saturday morning. "How do I know how I'll feel when Saturday rolls around?" she'd say. She'd never study until the night before a test. In her room after school she'd put on loud music and dance until her father carried the stereo from the room.

At the dinner table he'd point a finger at her, lecturing while their two older, more manageable children stared into their plates. "You can't just do things in this life when you want to." Kelly would roll her eyes. For him, life was a long-range project. He devoted himself to securing the future. When each child was born, he put one thousand dollars into a college fund. Kelly would have been in her junior year by now.

At times—when she felt bitter—Melanie thought how Hal hadn't minded Kelly's going so much as he minded her not leaving an itinerary. She thought he'd driven her away. But in her heart she knew this was not true. She had to blame herself as well. After Kelly left, Melanie spent months wondering what she'd done wrong. She thought of all the times she'd told Kelly to stop moving, to sit still. Kelly was different from the other children. She was different from all of them. They should have loved her for her differences, not tried to make her one of them.

Hal fell asleep on top of the RV's kitchen table, which converted into a double bed, but Melanie found it impossible to sleep. The rain had stopped, so she put a robe on and went outside. The air smelled fresh; now it was a clear starry night, and she stood at the side of the Winnebago at the edge of the road in her nightgown and robe, looking up at the stars. Then she sat down on a large rock, facing Head of Mother Earth

Mountain, whose silhouette she could see in the moonlight. She had no idea how long she sat. She was aware only of changes in the configuration of the stars, the place of the moon overhead. She was aware of the rock beneath her, turning warm. It seemed as if she could feel something flow within the rock. She loved the feel of the warm breeze against her skin and through her gown. She loved the clear sky overhead.

Melanie didn't notice the prowling of a coyote not that far away, or the flight overhead of an owl. She thought how beautiful it was there. What a beautiful country this was. They had gone out of their way and now they were lost. She thought of Kelly, spending night after night like this beneath the stars. She found herself suddenly as close to her daughter as she'd ever come. She felt as if she could sit there forever. As if she could just stay in that spot.

As the sun was starting to shine on the face of Head of Mother Earth Mountain, Hal opened the door and found her sitting on the rock. "What are you doing?" he shouted. Then he sat down beside her, putting his arm across her back. "Are you all right?"

She had no idea how long she had been there, but she was awakened as if from a dream. She felt refreshed, though she was not sure if she had slept. "I'm fine. I'm ready to go on."

The Winnebago started up with no problem, and they hadn't gone a thousand yards when they saw the single arrow, pointing straight ahead. And suddenly they arrived at a small stand with "Dinosaur tracks here" in the same scrawl they'd followed for so long painted in black letters on the side of the shack. An old woman sold beads. A man in a blue vest stood in the shade. His dark hair was greasy, parted to one side. His tired eyes widened as they approached. "I'll be your guide," the man said, "for five dollars."

Hal gave the man the five dollars, and they parked the van. They got out and followed him. "Over here," he said, "tracks of diplodocus and tyrannosaurus." They followed the man across the muddy clay. The old woman removed the shawl from her head. She was bald. Melanie could not even begin to guess her age. They walked for about two hundred yards across the desert and then the man stopped. "There," he said, pointing to the faint, wet imprints of a dinosaur's foot.

Melanie and Hal looked down. At first they could not see them. The tracks looked like ripples in the rock. But then the man drew the outline with his finger. "There," he said. At last they both recognized it. They stared into the wide, deep petrified dinosaur track. "Hey, Mel," Hal said, "get closer." He raised the videocam. Melanie thought how he looked like a lab technician, setting her up for an X-ray.

Melanie stepped to the right, then to the left. "Back a little," Hal said. The Indian looked at them strangely. Finally Melanie took one more step back, letting her feet sink into the red-clay water that filled the tyrannosaurus tracks. Hal stared at Melanie, her feet having disappeared. He put the videocam down, letting it drop to his side. She looked like a clown with giant feet. The clay soaked into her shoes. She thought how good it felt to have her feet in these clay tracks. How good it was to stand in the tracks of this creature who was gone.

THE
Moon Garden

When Jessie told her mother she was getting married, Mara began to dream. For years Mara's nights had been dark and uneventful, but now she dreamed the same dream that had come to her before Jessie was born. She dreamed that Jessie was a baby, a newborn. On the first day Mara cradled and nursed her. On the second day Jessie walked. On the third day she went to school. On the fourth day she went to high school, and on the fifth day Mara packed her off to college and she was gone. At the end of the dream Mara was always standing in the doorway of a house she'd never owned, handkerchief in hand, waving. Mara had thought before Jessie was born that the dream meant she didn't want to have a child. That it was a mistake.

Now the dream came back to her. Everything was the same except that the house Mara waved from was the one they had bought upstate just before Burt died, the house that was to be their weekend retreat, that had become her home.

Jessie had phoned to say, "Mom, guess what, I'm marrying Zach."

Mara had replied, only half-jokingly, "Who's Zach?"

"Oh, Mother," Jessie moaned, "you know."

Actually, Mara barely knew. She had met him only once or twice and then not for very long. She couldn't say if she disapproved of Jessie's marriage to Zach, a nice enough man who was going to be an architect, but she didn't exactly approve either. Certainly Zach wasn't the kind of man Jessie used to date, the ones whose spiked hair made them look like stegosaurs and who asked impertinent questions about Mara's accent and where she came from.

"Louisiana," she liked to respond to their inquiries. "The Blue Bayou." They'd look at her askance. In fact she'd come from Berlin via London and New York, but that was nobody's business but her own.

Mara knew it was hardly her place to approve or disapprove of Jessie's choices. Jessie had been making up her own mind since she was three years old, when she decided she wanted her hair cut short. Jessie's hair had been like honey—thick, pale, and flowing; it had been Mara's pride and joy. People stopped her in supermarkets, perfect strangers, and said, "Look at that child's hair. Isn't it wonderful?" Women gasped, saying, "Do you set those curls? Is that her natural color?" Once a man, an artist Mara assumed, lifted Jessie's hair into his hands. "Titian red," he had exclaimed.

Jessie had had the features to match. Eyes the color of green pools. Skin like pale fruit. An exquisite child who had been spared pain and grief. And then one day when she was just three, she said to her mother, "I want my hair short." Mara ignored this. What can a three-year-old know about having her hair cut? But then Jessie said it again and again. "I want short hair. Like my friends." So Mara had agreed. She'd taken Jessie to a Hispanic beauty shop in the Village, where the little girl sat on the phone books for Brooklyn, Manhattan, and Queens and told the lady to cut her hair short.

When the scissors were put to Jessie's hair, it was Mara who burst out crying, as if something more than hair was gone. Tears had welled in the eyes of the Spanish beauticians; the clientele as well. Even now Mara recalled how she had crawled on the floor, scooping clumps of hair into a plastic bag that she kept to this day in the back of her lingerie drawer, hair that she sometimes would take out and comb.

A few weeks after Jessie had called to say she was getting married, she'd called again. "Mother . . . ," Jessie said, a sheepish tone to her voice.

She's calling this off, Mara thought, relieved. Mara had been sitting up on those nights when her dream aroused her, thinking of how to make her daughter change her mind.

"Mother, Zach and I have been talking," Jessie spoke sweetly, the way she did when she wanted something, "and we were thinking that we'd like to be married at your place, in the garden."

"Here?" Mara said, trying to imagine her retreat in upstate New York deluged with design students from Cooper Union. "When?"

"In early June."

Mara peered down at her crocuses, hyacinths, daffodils, and tulips, all about to bloom. Ever since she and Burt had bought the place a decade ago, Mara had hoped Jessie would want to be married here. But not yet (she wasn't even twenty-five) and probably not to Zach. "In early June?"

"Yes, perhaps the first weekend. Why? Does it matter?"

"It isn't a good time."

"A good time for you?"

"No," Mara said, emphatically, as if this were absurd. "For the garden."

"The garden?" Jessie said.

"It'll be between blooms."

"I'm not sure I understand."

Mara thought of early June when the tops of the irises, tulips, and daffodils would be cut back, their leaves and stalks lying dormant as the bulbs absorbed the food they needed for the following year. The garden would be all brown, wilted, with no new blooms. "The spring flowers will have faded and the summer flowers won't be up. It won't have any color. Couldn't the wedding wait until July? It would be better then."

"Oh." Jessie paused. "Can't we just stick some annuals in? Petunias or something?"

"I suppose . . ." But Mara did not like this idea at all.

"We wanted to go away for the summer, Mom. We're going to see all the villas in Italy."

"Ah, Europe." Mara sighed, her voice far away. "Well, I'll have to think about it."

"Oh, you don't have to think about it," Jessie said. "We'll take care of everything."

In early April Jessie and Zach drove up in Zach's old van. Mara was stooped over, digging with her trowel in the cold, loamy soil. The ground was still hard. She had almost forgotten they were coming. When she saw them, for a moment she wondered who they were. Mara had met Zach only a couple of times and was never impressed, though she couldn't say why. She had trouble remembering his name. He was a second-year architecture graduate student at Cooper Union, whose senior project was a postmodernist design for a low-income housing project along the East River. She had no reason to dislike him.

He was, Mara had to admit, attractive, responsible, a little moody. But that was Jessie's problem, not hers. Still, she saw nothing special about him. Nothing that brought him clearly into focus in her mind.

"So here you are," Mara said as they walked out back.

"We thought we'd just sit down and plan it all together, Mom." Jessie looked tired, Mara thought, as she received her daughter's hug. Mara struggled to keep her dirty hands from touching Jessie. She glanced at their jeans, their sweaters and down vests, which made the two look as if they were modeling for a catalog. She was sure they'd made these purchases for this visit.

"Hello, Mara," Zach said, kissing her on the cheek. Had he ever called her Mara before?

Zach came from Tampa. He had grown up in the sun and had a weathered face, so different from Jessie's pale, New York features. He just wasn't what Mara had in mind.

First, he wasn't Jewish, which had never really mattered much before, but suddenly it mattered enormously. Had she survived all that she had so that her only living flesh and blood marry an Episcopalian graduate student? Shouldn't they perhaps stick to their own kind—not that Mara had ever thought about what this meant before. She had never really liked the notion of having your own kind.

Now she gazed at Jessie, whose coloring was still that of honey and peaches, though her hair had remained short. She was clinging to the arm of this rugged-looking man whom Mara had hardly ever laid eyes on, whom as far as she was concerned her daughter scarcely knew.

"We know this is rather short notice," Zach said.

"Yes, six weeks is rather short notice," Mara mused. "These will be all gone." She pointed to the tulips she had bought through a mail-order catalog from Holland, "and nothing will have replaced them."

"Well, we just want to do it," Jessie said, with the defiant pout Mara never liked, even when Jessie was very small and other people thought it was cute. "We don't want a big deal and we don't want to wait."

"I'll just finish up here," Mara said. "Why don't you go inside and rest from your drive."

Now Jessie's face relaxed and again she gave her mother a hug. "You shouldn't work so hard."

Mara watched them head back into the house. Then she turned back to her plants and to preparing the soil. Jessie, Mara thought, didn't understand the essential things. An interior designer, she knew nothing about the outdoors. It had been a mistake, trying to raise a child in a small New York apartment. Jessie knew how to move a wall or put in a thousand shelves where none had been before, or make a room that faced an air shaft appear light, but she knew nothing of the earth, the weather patterns, the timing of blooms.

Early June was the worst time of year for the garden. The primroses would be going (she was lucky to have them at all in this climate). The roses wouldn't have bloomed. The day lilies, which made a carpet of orange and yellow, would not be up yet. Mid-May, of course, was the nicest time for spring flowers, as was late June for summer blossoms. But early June just wouldn't do.

There was a solution to which Mara did not want to agree, but it was viable. She could plant a special garden for the occasion. She could cut back her tulips to the ground, which she hated to do, and plant just annuals. She could move some of the perennials to another part of the garden, the whole of which was quite big now, for Mara had worked on it almost exclusively since she left her publishing job five years ago.

She'd worked as a copy editor, correcting spelling and factual errors. But continuity was her specialty. She could read a five-hundred-page manuscript and know if a character had blue eyes on page three and green eyes on page four hundred. Or if someone drank vodka tonics, then switched for no reason to whiskey. When Mara was done with a book, one could be sure that the characters were consistent and historical events happened in sequence.

It was continuity that made her garden special as well, for she knew how to move from season to season. Except for June, her transitions were always smooth.

For years Mara had contemplated a theme garden. A showplace that would be dramatically different from her carefully planned one of perennial blooms. She had thought about edible flowers or Cajun blooms; an English garden or wildflowers. She'd even considered a sinister garden once, one that would sprout only poisonous plants. Mara paused, smiling at this possibility for the wedding, then discarded it. She could plant an all-green garden. Or a moon garden. It was something she had wanted to try.

A pure white garden of white snaps, baby's breath, white roses, white mums, white hydrangeas. Candytuft for ground cover. And moonflower, that strange morning glory that opens only at night. A garden that shimmered in the moonlight. She could do this, but the thought of everything white frightened her.

After Jessie and Zach showered and had a nap (Mara listened for the telltale signs of sheets rustling, but the two were discreet), they all sat down to discuss the wedding plans. The first thing Jessie announced was, instead of gifts, they'd asked their friends to bring food.

"A potluck?" Mara mused.

"That's what we really want from our friends. A great meal."

"Please," Mara said, "I'll get a caterer." Jessie and Zach demurred. Mara assumed they'd fight this battle again at a later date. Actually she didn't much care; her thoughts were elsewhere. "Now I was thinking, if you could get married just a few weeks later . . ."

"We can't. We just can't. Right, Zach?"

Zach nodded dumbly. Mara glanced at him. It occurred to her that maybe this was all Jessie's idea. Maybe Zach didn't want to be married at all. Jessie seemed adamant, but perhaps Zach was not. Perhaps if she could get him alone, she could win him over. Talk him out of it. "A few weeks would make such a difference, for the garden."

Jessie rubbed her eyes in an exasperated way. Jessie thinks I'm aging, turning strange, Mara thought to herself. I'm diminished, a shadow of what I used to be. An old fuddy-duddy.

"Mom, you spend hours, months on your garden." Jessie turned to Zach. "She won't even let anyone touch it. I'm sure it will be fine."

"It will not be fine and you are my only flesh and blood and I'm not having just any old flower patch for your wedding. Do you understand?"

Jessie rolled her eyes. "Let's not make this complicated."

"But it is complicated," Mara said. "Growing seasons are complicated. When things bloom is complicated. I've spent years on this." Silently she lamented, though she could not say this to them, that her bridal veil astilbe wouldn't flower until late June. And, of course, that was the one she wanted most of all.

She saw Jessie glance at Zach and he nodded back. She knew they had anticipated this. That she would behave in this way. "This matters to me," she found herself shouting, then shaking her head. They stared at her. They knew nothing.

It was her mother who had taught Mara about gardening. She could see her now. A trim, elegant woman with hair the same color as Jessie's, in a dress, bent over their garden in Berlin. It had been magnificent, not like this small garden Mara grew. It was huge, or so she remembered it, with all kinds of blooming trees, trees that bore fruit that Mara could reach up and pluck in their season. Giant roses that smelled for months at a time. Mara could remember as a girl running among the falling petals of the blooming trees in the spring, laughing, while her mother paused from her digging, looking up at Mara to smile.

Sometimes her mother would take her by the hand. Mara could still see her mother's fingers—raw, sore, dirt under the nails. Mara had loved her mother's rough touch, the calloused fingers that held her. At dinner her father would hold up her mother's hands and shake his head—this elegant woman with her hands raw. Her mother always pulled them away. She would never wear gloves, she told him. She loved to feel her hands in the ground, digging. "I just can never get them clean," she'd say, laughing.

Then the war came and they had to leave everything behind. Mara's mother had wept for days, for weeks. They moved into a flat in London with cousins. They were safe, but when spring came there was no garden, nowhere to plant. Mara's mother sat staring at her hands, wondering what to do with them. Sometimes Mara saw her father hold them, but nothing seemed to matter. That spring it was cold and there was little heat. Mara wasn't sure how long her mother lingered after she became sick, but remembered that at the time she died, her hands were very clean.

Her father was never really the same after that. Mara was raised by her cousins, unhappy people who never smiled. She left home as soon as she was able. But sometimes at night, even now, Mara imagined her mother, sitting, holding her hand. Or at the foot of the bed, telling her a bedtime story. At times she sensed her mother's presence in the room, but of course she could tell this to no one. Even after she'd married Burt, she felt her mother's presence hovering over her bed. Once she'd called out in the night, calling her by name, to Burt's dismay.

Though Mara married him, Burt was not the man she had loved. That man was Sam, an American she had met after the war and followed to New York. He too had died, but not of a broken heart. He had been killed by a drunken driver on a

Saturday night as they drove along the parkway. They were heading to a meadow to make love in the moonlight. He had died instantly and Mara had walked away without a scratch, dazed.

She married Burt because she was getting old and because her family in England was beginning to worry about her and because her money was running out and Burt was a CPA. He was a nice man with a gentle disposition. Though he had idiosyncrasies, such as a refusal to eat Chinese food, to travel except to Florida (and the Gulf Coast at that), and to let anyone but himself fix anything in his house (hence some things never got repaired), Mara had never disliked him. But she had never loved him either.

And then Jessie was born. Just when Mara thought that every little corner of her heart where feelings might grow was dead, Jessie came and Mara found herself consumed. Though she remained married, she discarded Burt like an empty husk, a rind. She hovered over the child, amazed at her every move, living in dread that something would happen. When Jessie first suckled at Mara's breast, Mara thought, so this is it. This is what it is all about. To want so much you will break.

None of this Mara had ever told Jessie. The real story she held safely within. Sometimes Mara was amazed that the world looked the same, that people went about their business, their lives, after all that had happened.

"I think," Mara said, "we should do wildflowers. They're interesting. And they have a disheveled look to them, something you'd like, I think." Jessie and Zach contemplated this. A disheveled look. They glanced at their jeans, their hands. They looked at each other.

"Of course, they're unpredictable," Mara added.

"Mom, whatever you feel like. Whatever you think works. I'm sure it will be fine." Mara knew what Jessie wanted. She wanted her mother to stop thinking about this.

"You don't understand," Mara said, looking into their doubting faces, their inscrutable eyes. "I want it to be beautiful. I want you to have all the beautiful things in this world."

That afternoon Jessie and Mara drove into town to buy supplies for dinner. It was one of the things they did well together—cook. They liked to make roasts and big vegetable casseroles, bustling around one another in the kitchen. Though they were both thin, they loved a hearty meal and had the same taste in food. That evening it would be brisket, roasted potatoes, a bean casserole, a huge salad.

In the car Jessie spoke first, but Mara was disappointed for it was what she broached each time she came to visit or called from the cavernous hallways of Cooper Union, always collect. "Mother," she said, "I'm worried about you. Who do you talk to? What do you do?"

"I talk to myself," Mara teased.

She and Burt had bought the house as a weekend retreat, but Burt had died suddenly on his way to work, a heart attack, at the age of fifty. He'd left everything to Mara and Jessie. With what little there was, Mara could make do. She continued to work for a few years, but finally she realized that if she gave up one place—either the apartment in the city or this house where she now lived—she could make ends meet. She gave up her job and the apartment and made the country her full-time residence without batting an eye.

"Well, that's what I'm afraid of," Jessie said. "You shouldn't be so far away. I think you should move back down to the city. You like concerts and museums, people."

"Right, and crime, filth, pollution . . ."

"Well, then, move closer. Long Island. Nyack."

"Jessie, I like it here. I'm happy. I don't need the city. I'm fifty-five and this is fine for me. There's a bunch of old ladies and artists and we all keep to ourselves, but I've got people if I want them. And I can do whatever I want. I like the country, the house, the garden. I'm happy here."

Jessie thought about this for a moment. "And in winter. In winter you tend the garden?"

"Winter, spring, summer, fall, I tend the garden."

"Mother, you're getting weirder and weirder."

"You should talk, my dear," remembering the black leather outfit Jessie had worn the last time she visited.

"You're my mother and I don't know you at all."

Mara pondered this for a while. "You know what you need to know."

"You think so, but I don't." Mara heard the exasperation in Jessie's voice. "Maybe I'd like to have dinner with you once in a while," Jessie said, trying to change the tone.

"It's only a three-hour drive. You can come for a weekend."

"It's not the same, Mother. It's just not the same."

"We each have our lives. You make your choices. I'll make mine."

Jessie, Mara thought, had had her own share of difficulties. She had dropped out of high school to study at an actors' studio in the Village and had gotten pregnant. Burt had disowned her—the only stand he had ever taken was against his own daughter. And Jessie had stubbornly, perhaps only to spite him, decided to keep the child. When she miscarried on a cold winter's night, Mara had rushed to New York Hospital and held her eighteen-year-old daughter's hand as Jessie delivered a still-born child. The doctor had said, "Do you want to see it?"

"You don't need to see it," Mara told Jessie. "You don't need to look."

Jessie had gone on from that and put her life back together. Finished high school, got into Cooper Union on the basis of her portfolio alone, only to throw it all away now. Jessie always does what she wants, Mara thought. She always has.

"I'm sorry," Mara said, "but I just don't know what you see in Zach."

"I love him, Mother. Isn't that enough?"

Mara shook her head. Then she was silent for the rest of the drive home.

Zach had the table set and was reading *War and Peace* when they returned.

"*War and Peace?*" Mara exclaimed.

"It relaxes me," Zach replied. "Can I help you with dinner?"

He is only reading this book to impress me, she thought. "No thank you, we don't need any help."

"Oh, she never wants any help. Mom, why don't you just relax." Jessie laughed, pushing her mother gently toward the stairs. "We'll take care of dinner."

Mara didn't want to relax. What she wanted to do was cook dinner with her daughter. But mostly she wanted to do things. Keep busy. She wanted to feel the motion of her hands, chopping, scraping. Dejected, she went outside. Through the window she could see the two of them, heads bowed, as they cut and diced together, speaking in whispers. About her, she imagined. They were talking about her. How would they manage her. Perhaps even now they were making their minds up to elope.

Mara looked at her garden. The tulips would soon be in full bloom. She loved the splashes of color, all of which she had carefully planned. If her life had taken a different turn, she would have been a painter. A female Manet or Gauguin. Traveling to exotic places or simply remaining in a garden of her own choosing, lush, exuberant, full of color. If her life had been different, her parents would have sent her to study in Paris.

Sometimes Mara painted. She sketched the trees, the flowers, but her real gift, she knew, was with the living things themselves.

A tap at the window aroused her. She saw Jessie, her face pressed foolishly to the glass, as she'd done as a child, her face flattened like a clown.

They ate potatoes, brisket, beans almost in silence. Jessie

made small talk about her work. This was the first meal the three of them had actually had together, and Zach appeared to have been briefed. He asked Mara innocuous questions— "Don't you miss the city?" or "Was it difficult, raising a child and having a career?"—the kind of direct questions young people might ask of those they think are very old, as if to pamper them. At least he wasn't rude. He didn't pry; he asked nothing that made her cringe or forced her to lie.

Mara didn't want to eat, but she made herself. She didn't want to talk either, and after a while Zach gave up. Jessie said she was tired just as they were done and excused herself.

"Do you mind?" She touched Zach on the shoulder. "I want to take a bath."

"No." He patted her hand. "I'll clean up."

Mara was surprised it had come so easily—their moment alone. Now she could talk to him, speak to him sensibly about how there was no reason to rush into marriage if he wasn't completely sure. How there would be plenty of time after graduate school. She was about to say something when she noticed his hand. It was true she had met him only a couple of times, so it was possible to miss such a flaw. But hands were something Mara usually noticed. As he was folding his fingers around her plate, she saw that the index finger of his right hand was missing.

"Done, Mara?" he asked.

"You're missing your finger," she said.

"That's right, I am."

Mara rose from the table and followed him into the kitchen. "What happened?"

Zach laughed and shook his head. "Oh, it's a crazy story. You don't want to know."

"Yes, I do." Mara nodded.

Zach leaned against the counter. "I was a little boy in Tampa, playing outside. You know, the kinds of things kids do. I saw something in the bushes. It was quite beautiful. I remember that. It had beautiful colors and I reached for it. A coral snake bit my finger."

Mara shook her head. "It bit your finger off?"

Zach stared at her, surprised, it seemed, that he'd gotten her attention. "No, it didn't bite it off. My neighbor chopped it off." He put down the plates. "You see, a coral snake has a very deadly but slow poison. Once it starts to travel, there's not much you can do. My neighbor saw me running around with this snake attached to my finger, and he knew what it was right away. He was a doctor, and he just took a butcher knife and"— Zach made a chopping motion with his hand that made Mara flinch—"that was it."

Mara went up to him, touching his hand, turning the stump this way and that. Zach did not pull away. She tried to imagine this stranger who slept with her daughter, who planned to marry her, this graduate student with sandy brown hair, in a garden with a snake clinging to his finger. "And you learned to write, to draw?"

"Yes," he said slowly, "I learned to do everything."

"How strange."

"Not to me," Zach said. "I've lived with this a long time now."

"No, it's strange that I never noticed it before," Mara muttered, wondering what other things she had never noticed. What else had she missed that was before her eyes? This thought troubled her and for a long time she held his hand.

Jessie came into the kitchen, her hair wrapped in a towel, her face red and flushed, and saw Mara holding her fiancé's hand.

"What is it?" she asked.

Mara looked up, embarrassed. "Well. I just never noticed . . ."

"Your mother has taken an interest in my missing finger."

"Oh really," Jessie said.

"I have all my fingers," Mara said, holding up her hand.

"Most people do," Zach said.

"Did it hurt?"

"The snakebite?"

"No, when your neighbor cut it off."

"I think it hurt my dad more." Zach laughed. "He had to hold me down. I don't think he's ever gotten over it. He carried that finger around with him for days, trying to get someone to sew it back on. Then he buried it in the garden. I remember he cried. He watched over me like a maniac for years after that."

So other parents are like me, Mara thought. They go wild.

They can't bear their children's pain. They hold on when they should let go.

That night Mara slept soundly until something made her stir. A breeze, her dream, a fleeting thought. It made her get up and go to the window. What had woken her?

She peered down across the fields in the moonlight and then down to the wall in the garden where she saw Jessie and Zach. They were speaking in whispers, so that their voices could not have disturbed her. Mara tried to imagine what they were talking about. Her fascination with his finger? Serpents in the garden? All the good the world has known? Or about something mundane. The guest list, Jessie's dress, the hill towns of Italy they would visit.

The moon was almost full. Perhaps it was the light that had woken her. In it Mara saw Zach take Jessie's arm and pull her to him, not to kiss her, but just to have her near. It was a simple gesture, but somehow it moved Mara almost to tears. Then Jessie turned into Zach's body and lay against him. They walked, pressed together. In the moonlight they appeared white as if they were naked and cold.

Once she had watched her own parents from the window of her room on a warm summer's night, and they had walked in the garden like this. Mara had thought, even then as a little girl, how something palpable flowed between them. And it had been that way for her with Sam. Decades ago. It had been like that when they'd driven on weekends when the moon was high, to a meadow to make love.

Now Mara watched Jessie and Zach, their faces in shadows, walking in the garden. The trees and flowers, the lilacs especially, were redolent. They floated like ghosts.

She watched as they headed toward the wall. They were going out into the fields. But for an instant before disappearing they paused, intertwined, standing perfectly still, shimmering like a tree in the moonlight.

THE
Glass-Bottom Boat

Lenore sat on the plastic lounge chair, listening to the wind. Except for the young lovers a few chairs down who were nestled under a hotel blanket and the very fat couple who stared straight ahead, she was the only person out. The wind had picked up the night before when the air was cool, but suddenly it turned muggy and strong, a south wind that blew the scents of hibiscus and wild ginger out of the air and made the islanders smirk when the tourists asked, "How much longer do you think it will last?"

Lenore had noticed this smirk after she'd asked three or four people because already the girls were getting antsy. They could play video games and roll around on a mat at Woody's Day Camp for a few hours a day, but after that, Lenore had to improvise. Aunt Patty, who ran the day camp, said that a pony named Angel was supposed to come and give the kids rides, but Angel didn't like the wind.

Lenore didn't like it either. It didn't bring rain and there were no signs of an oncoming storm, but the palm trees were tilted at odd angles and the fronds slapped like an audience impatient for the show to begin. The wind didn't have the excitement of a storm or the promise of something untamed and dramatic that would carry itself across the island and out to sea. It just blew sand in faces, skirts into the air, clothing off the lines. It made people act strange. Earlier, when she'd tried to take a walk up the beach, she'd passed a tall, thin black man, dancing. He swayed back and forth, his eyes closed, moving his feet as if to a calypso beat, but there was no music. Then she'd headed over to the lounge chair where she now sat.

Lenore, Marty, and the girls had arrived on Wednesday for their one-week package (sixteen hundred including meals; children ate free). A week on the islands, sipping papaya drinks and piña coladas. They'd chosen the Holiday Inn because Marty wanted "a familiar face in an exotic place." He didn't mind walking up the road for a ham-and-cheese sandwich or to bargain for a T-shirt from the duty-free shops. He'd even tried the jerk chicken at the evening buffet, but he didn't want things to be too different from what he was used to. "I'm a what-you-see-is-what-you-get kind of guy," Marty liked to say.

They had had two days of sunshine and their twin daughters—Crystie with the beautiful hair and Claire with the beautiful voice (this was how people told them apart, as if they were characters in a fairy tale)—had ridden the paddleboats and snorkeled and even tried windsurfing, though they were only nine. They had pleaded with their mother to take them out on the glass-bottom boat and Lenore had gone along reluctantly because she'd never done well in deep water and once she'd almost drowned.

The next day the wind had started. It had blown the people inside. It blew panties and bathing suits drying on balconies off to sea; it blew coffee cups cold and beach chairs across lawns. As Lenore sat by the pool, she saw a cat fly across the deck and into the bushes where it disappeared.

From her lounge chair Lenore could see into rooms. Babies were confined to their cribs, parents gazed hopelessly at board games and portable video games. Tourists huddled in unmade beds, reading dimestore novels whose pages were sodden with moisture from the sea wind. She saw feet draped across beds, empty glasses on nightstands. Faces peered out of closed curtains, scanning the sky.

She hadn't slept well the night before because the people in the next room were having a party. She'd heard their music and laughter and finally she'd woken Marty, who was a light sleeper but hadn't heard a thing. She'd asked him to do something about what was going on next door, but when he went to knock, everything quieted down.

That morning Lenore had gone to the front desk to complain. She was unhappy with her room, she'd told the desk clerk, a dark, indifferent man. She said the people next door were too noisy. The desk clerk punched something into his computer, then told her that he was glad to change her room, but that the room next door to theirs was unoccupied. "That can't be," Lenore said. "I heard people there."

The desk clerk looked at her wide-eyed, askance. "It's under construction," the man said. "It doesn't even have furniture." He offered to give her a key so she could see for herself, and with a defiant look she snatched it from him. Without telling Marty, she went to the room next door and turned the key. She'd walked into an empty space with a green blanket over the window, a cement floor, and a housekeeping cart with clean towels in the middle of the room. She had quickly closed the door.

Now she sat on the lounge chair, the key still in her pocket. She touched its impression to make sure it was there. She'd planned to return it, but decided to do it later. The fruit lady came by—papaya, coconut, mango in a basket on her head, a cleaver in her fist. Lenore asked her to smash a coconut which she'd take back to the girls. "Sounds like a hurricane, doesn't it?" Lenore said.

The fruit lady looked at Lenore with disdain as she lowered the basket from her head. Lenore watched as the woman removed the coconut and cracked it with a firm whack right across the side. "No," the fruit lady said, "this is just wind. When it's a hurricane, the air whistles like this." And she made such a screeching sound that Lenore put her hands over her ears.

━━━━━━

The glass-bottom boat couldn't go out because of the wind. In fact, all beach activities were suspended until further notice. There was no windsurfing, no paddleboats. As Lenore broke the news, the girls shrieked, "Oh, Mommy, our vacation is ruined." Marty headed out to the bar to watch CNN because there were no TVs in the rooms. This was intended, Marty had surmised, to keep the guests outside, renting water-front equipment or drinking at the bar where the TV was always on. The girls slumped on their bed, faces buried in their pillows, pretending to cry. But Lenore was secretly relieved.

The boat was a simple skiff, the kind they'd rented in Wisconsin one summer, except this one had a dirty glass-paneled floor. Claire and Crystie had, of course, loved it as the boat sailed above sea grass and reefs where they looked down on mushroom and elkhorn and fire coral whose touch produced acid burns. They'd squealed as the boat glided over spotted eels and camouflage fish, brain coral, and those iridescent blue fish, the jewels of the sea, and the one long gray fish that Gosset, the disgruntled Jamaican boat operator, said was not a shark.

But while the girls cried in delight, Lenore felt a sense of panic as she stared into the dark opening above a murky green sea. It was the same feeling she'd once had when she'd gotten stuck in an elevator in the Central Illinois Bank building. Even though she'd known help was on the way, she'd had to fight for air. On the glass-bottom boat her heart had started pounding and she couldn't catch her breath. Later that night the wind had started and her pain—the mysterious pain that crept from her neck down her shoulder into her arm—the pain she had almost come to believe was gone, returned.

Then Claire lost her voice. She had a voice that sang as sweetly as meadowlarks after a rain, but that morning she'd woken up and whispered, "Mommy, I can't speak." While she was relegated to silence, Crystie's silken strands turned to a Brillo-like frizz. As Claire scribbled notes in a child's hand— "I'm bored," or "I'm hungry, let's eat"—Crystie sobbed in the bathroom as she tried to comb out the snarls.

Now the girls picked up their Aladdin video game and Lenore snapped at them. "Put it on mute," she said, heading into the bathroom where she squeezed T-shirts and socks that she'd hung on the clothesline two days before that were still wet. She heard the girls squabbling and she didn't want to be in the room. Next time they'd splurge and get two rooms, but then who ever thought that on a vacation in Jamaica you'd be stuck inside.

Crystie wanted to go to Woody's Day Camp to see if Angel the pony was going to show, but Claire just wanted to walk the shore, so they dropped Crystie off and trudged along the paved walkway that followed the beach, their faces wincing in the wind. They passed a tall black man in khaki pants, cutting the hedges with a machete. He was humming to himself as he sheared off the tops with smooth, even strokes, but as they walked by, he looked up and said hello, smiling through white, shiny teeth. Lenore wondered as she smiled back if he wasn't the same man she'd seen earlier that morning, the one dancing to no music. This man was long and thin as a drinking straw and his skin was creamy like chocolate. Claire croaked back, "Hello."

"What's wrong with your voice?" the man asked.

And Lenore told him. "She lost it."

"Oh, it's the damp and the wind. You need the milk of a green coconut. You drink that. And then you need to make an herb tea with banana seeds. Boil it nice and hot; it will cure her overnight." He extended his hand, a gesture that surprised Lenore. His palm was pink and she was startled by its rough touch. "My name is Erroll," he said. "After Erroll Flynn, the famous pirate."

"Oh, yes," Lenore said, "Captain Blood. He was a bad man, wasn't he?"

Erroll grinned. He had a wide mouth, nice teeth. "My mother didn't think so."

"Well, where can we get the green coconut?" Lenore asked. Erroll smiled again, pointing overhead. Lenore watched as he wrapped his arms around the trunk of the coconut palm and shimmied up it. His khaki pants slid along the tree and Lenore thought, though she'd never say this, that he looked just like a monkey without a tail. He chopped down a green coconut and it fell to the sand with a thud. Then he used the tip of his machete to pierce a hole in the top and he told Claire to hold the coconut back and drink it, that it would taste watery and sweet as mother's milk. He told her not to try to say anything for twelve hours. In the meantime he would bring her the herbs and banana seed. In the morning, he said, she would speak.

Then he noticed Lenore rubbing her neck where the pain

was working its way down. "You've got something wrong with you, too," Erroll said. He stared at them with a look of concern. He said that maybe the white witch had cast a spell on them. Lenore couldn't tell if he was kidding or not. She was a white woman, he told them, who'd killed her husband when he betrayed her with a black woman. Her duppy is around here, he said. You know a duppy because of the white mist that moves along the ground like a cloud, rising slowly in the air. Salt, he told her, keeps the soul heavy and on the ground. That was why black people couldn't go back to Africa: because the slaves ate salt. Everyone knows that African people can fly; it's the salt that keeps them down.

L enore had dreamed of this vacation all her life. She had never been anywhere. Not to Europe or even to California. Sometimes they went to St. Louis to the zoo, and once they'd taken the girls to Disney World, but that was about it. Usually they put their money into fixing up the house. Last year they'd added on a family room with wood paneling and a little bar with recessed lighting. Even though Marty had done all the finishing work himself, they'd had to take out a home-improvement loan.

But Lenore wanted to go to Jamaica. When she was a girl, her mother had moved dreamily through the house, singing Harry Belafonte songs. Her mother was half in love with Harry Belafonte, but she would have slapped Lenore's face if she'd so much as suggested it. She'd slapped her face many times for much less.

When Lenore got back to their room, the twins in tow, she found Marty, red as a lobster, naked and splayed on the bed. Startled, he quickly pulled the cover across him. "Daddy's got a sunburn," the twins crooned.

"I told you to put on thirty-five," Lenore scolded. "I bet you put on sixteen."

"There's no sun," Marty protested. "Look, it's all over-cast."

"That's the worst kind for someone with your skin." Lenore plopped down next to Marty, rubbing her neck, hoping he would notice and massage it for her. When he didn't, she patted him on the leg, making him wince. "Come on," she said, wondering how a man who knows he burns can let himself burn. "Let's get something to eat."

They hadn't crossed the road yet but now because of the wind Lenore convinced them to get away from the shore. She'd heard from Aunt Patty that there was a good deli in the small row of shops just beyond the security gates. Across the road was different from their side of the road, where they had bought ham-and-cheese sandwiches from little stands. On the other side, reggae poured from the shops and along the curb, where rows of black men sat. Men with gold teeth and shells around their necks. The minute they saw Lenore, Marty, and the girls, the men all leapt to their feet. "Hey, Man, take a ride in my cab. I'll take you to the falls." "Hey, Man, buy your duty-free gold right here. Gold and silver. Pirate's treasure, Man.'' And when it became apparent that Lenore and Marty and the girls weren't going to buy anything except lunch, the shouts became jeers, ''Hey, Lobster Man, I take you to the clambake.''

The deli was in a small grocery store down a narrow path lined with shops that sold Aunt Jemima dolls and Bob Marley tapes, both of which the girls wanted, but Lenore said they'd have to wait. Inside the deli, which smelled of coconut oil and peppers, it was difficult to find the line. Swarms of people, mostly black, though a few tourists appeared from time to time, stood around the counter, buying curried goat, jerk pork. Lenore thought the conch fritters looked good. Marty pointed to pale strips of meat in a reddish sauce. ''What's that? Baked armadillo?'' The girls laughed, but Lenore shook her head.

Though they tried to hold their place, they seemed to be moving farther and farther away from the counter as more people arrived, butting in front of them. Then they pushed their way back up to the front, only to drift again toward the back. They finally made it to the counter when someone else cut in front of them. ''Hell of a lot of nerve,'' Marty cursed under his breath. Lenore sighed, watching Marty grow irate, which he rarely did, and which, of course, she couldn't blame him for now.

There were things she could never get used to either here. At breakfast when they asked if she wanted cream, they meant milk, but never bothered to explain. They never smiled when she changed money, and in the pharmacy she'd seen the salesgirl refuse to do an even exchange for a boy's triple-A batteries for double-A's. People danced when there was no music. And nobody waited in line.

Marty was about to tell the man who'd just cut in front of him that they were here first when Lenore realized it was Erroll. He turned to her with his wide-toothed grin and said, "You gotta let them know what you want," he said. "Don't nobody wait in line. Hey, Man," Erroll shouted to a woman working in a white apron, "take care of my friends." Then he ordered for them. Lenore watched the woman behind the counter fill take-out containers with peas and rice, conch fritters, curried goat, fried chicken for the girls.

Marty and Lenore thanked Erroll as they headed back across the road toward the iron gates of their hotel complex. They nodded at the security guard, who pushed a button and the gates parted slowly. Lenore heard feet behind her, scurrying to get in, and when she turned she saw Erroll again. "Is that guy following us or what?" Marty asked, walking on.

"He works here," Lenore said. Erroll was just a few paces behind them, carrying a small brown bag that didn't look like lunch; he strode with his head down as if he had something to hide. It occurred to Lenore that he was following them. She dropped back and asked if there was something he wanted. He said, keeping his head down, "I brought you this."

She opened the brown bag and saw tufts of grass, bits of bark. The smell of cedar closets and something rotting like a dead mouse wafted her way. "Boil it," he told her. "Make a good stiff tea. It'll take your pain away." Many doctors had tried to diagnose her pain. Some thought it was a slipped disk, though nothing ever showed up on the MRI. Others said it was arthritis, but she had tested negative for that as well. The pain just came and went as it wanted, like a casual lover. She figured she may as well try this. Quickly, she closed the bag and gave Erroll two dollars, for which he seemed grateful.

When they got to their room, Marty eased his way down on the edge of the bed, his sunburn making it so he had to sit with his arms and legs outstretched like a mummy, and ate his rice with peas and yams. The girls gobbled the fried chicken while Lenore sampled the curried goat, which she decided wasn't unlike stewed chicken. When he finished, Marty was still hungry, and he saw the paper bag on the nightstand. He opened it and took a whiff. "What is this stuff?" he asked, assuming it was something the girls had collected. Then he dropped it into the trash.

That night Lenore lay down beside Marty, whose sunburn was hot all around her, and she felt like a waffle. She'd wanted to make love once the girls were asleep, but he'd flinched at her touch. For a long time she lay beside him, thinking there was something she'd forgotten to do before she left home. A bill she hadn't paid, an automatic timer (thermostat, lights) she hadn't set.

When she started worrying about pipes freezing, she eased her way out of bed, went down to the beach bar, and ordered a rum punch. The man who sat beside her was a dead ringer for her ex-husband, Frank, whom she hadn't seen, nor wished to see, for twelve years. She had been married to him for only six months. He was the nicest man in the world until their honeymoon when they sat in a restaurant overlooking the Blue Ridge Mountains and he told her that she was a stupid little shit—it was downhill from there.

Marty was only a friend then. They worked at the same high school; he taught industrial arts and she taught special ed. Lenore worked with the learning-disabled in the local school district—children who read backwards, upside down, who could not follow a sequence. She devised tests for herself and for the teachers on her staff to show what it was like for the learning-disabled child—words with no vowels, words backwards.

When Lenore told Marty over coffee in the cafeteria that she thought Frank might hurt her, he moved her out of the house. He told Frank as unambivalently as he could that he would kill him if he ever came near her again. He had rescued her and she was thankful, though she wondered if gratitude was the best emotion to feel toward her husband.

Marty had smooth, wonderful hands, and he could make anything with them. Lenore thought it was good for someone to have one remarkable trait, and Marty's was what he could do with his hands. They used to make her shudder. She could lose herself in his hands. When the twins were born, he made them little lamps out of toy boats, and when they bought their house, he made door knockers that he poured himself from bronze.

Except for the incident with Frank, which she attributed to a lapse of judgment, she had lived an orderly life and she really had little to complain about. Now she kept staring at the man beside her until he stared back at her and said, ''Is something wrong?''

"No," she replied, as she paid her bill. And though she knew it sounded corny, she said, "You just remind me of someone I once knew." The man grinned, assuming it was a come-on, and went back to his drink.

Later when she crawled back in bed, Lenore found herself overwhelmed with the desire to touch someone. It didn't seem to matter much who the person was, but she just wanted to touch someone. She tried to determine the shape and gender of the person she longed to touch, but she couldn't quite make it out. It wasn't Marty, she was sure of that. Not that she didn't want to touch Marty, but it wasn't what she wanted now. When she was fifteen, she had made love to a boy once. She had lain with him on a blanket near one of the lakes and she felt as if her body would melt into his. She couldn't remember that boy's name, but she remembered what it felt like, to melt into someone else.

Lenore heard the noise of the people next door again. The party was in full swing; she heard laughter, dancing, and finally she could stand it no longer. It was the help, she decided, having a party after hours. She still had the key to the room and went to turn it in the lock but the door was already ajar. She pushed it open and found the room as it had been earlier that day: empty, devoid of furniture, the housekeeping cart in the center. But the green curtain by the window was pushed back. When she looked outside, Lenore could see a white mist rising from the lawn.

———

In the morning the wind was blowing as hard as before and Claire still could not speak. Crystie's hair was a nest of frizz and Marty's sunburn was hot enough to fry an egg on. The T-shirts and shorts she'd hung on the line in the bathroom were as wet as when she'd hung them days before. Waves hammered at the shore and, though the girls complained bitterly, they still could not go to the beach. Lenore convinced them that they should get a car and see the sights.

At the taxi stand they found a group of drivers, standing together in front of the hotel. Some had Rasta curls or wore little hats like tea cozies. Erroll was standing with them beside a banged-up car with pony upholstery and bronzed baby shoes dangling from the mirror. "Today is my day off," he said. "I'll take you around." A brief haggling went on among the drivers, speaking in patois, and then it was decided that it would be okay for Erroll to take them.

Lenore realized that Marty did not recognize Erroll from the day before, so she tugged at her husband's sleeve and said that she thought he had offered them a good price. They piled into his car. The windows were permanently fixed half-shut and the door on the passenger side could not be opened, so Marty had to go in on the driver's side and squeeze past the wheel. "I'll show you the caves first," Erroll said. "The girls will like the caves." He followed the coast—a clear, long stretch of developments, condos, and hotels—until they came to a place where the hotels seemed to stop. Here they parked at a beach where waterfall tumbled upon waterfall, and all the rivers that crisscrossed the island met—there was a tremendous crash of water all around. A dead pig floated in one of the pools at the base of the falls.

They took off their shoes and stripped down to the bathing suits they wore underneath, leaving their clothes in neat piles in the sand, and Erroll led them into the cave at the edge of the sea. It was a dark, green cave, cool and luminous inside, and the water was an iridescent blue. The girls made fish shadows on the wall. They floated on their backs as if they were asleep. Lenore found it so restful in the darkness, away from the wind, that she too wanted to go to sleep.

Erroll motioned for her to follow him deeper into the blue darkness of the cave. They went down a narrow passageway and came to a place where the walls shimmered like emeralds and the room was illumined with a phosphorescent green light, made by little animals, he told her. The air through the passage-way was warmer and more humid and Lenore had trouble catching her breath. She thought fleetingly of the elevator she'd once been trapped in, but she didn't feel that way now. It was more that the air seemed to thicken and grow heavy around her. Lenore could not see Erroll clearly, but she could make out his shadow. She heard his breathing. It was a shallow, rapid breath, as if he too were fighting for air. She could smell him. He smelled of spices and coconut and goat. She had never touched a black person's skin before, but now she wanted to touch his. She thought it would be soft, like a child's.

Listening to his breathing, she wondered if he would reach out and touch her. Otherwise, why did he bring her farther into the cave? She didn't know why she thought this, but she did. Lenore wanted something to happen. She didn't know what it was she wanted, but this was her vacation. She wanted it to be different from her life. She saw him ahead of her now; she could just make out a blue-black specter, looming before her. Then Erroll stepped closer and she felt his breath on her throat. "We should leave now," he whispered. He told her that two boys had drowned there once, caught in a tide that pressed them against the walls. Lenore shuddered, rubbing her neck.

She followed him back through the passageway where they found the girls, still making fish shadows on the walls, and Marty taking a picture. "It's time to go," Erroll said. When they left the cave they squinted in the light and were met with the full force of the wind, pushing them, blowing them back. Marty said he couldn't stand the wind anymore so Erroll offered to drive them inland, away from the sea, where the wind would be better. "I will show you my town," he said. "There is a small market there if you would like to buy a few things."

Lenore didn't want to buy anything, though she thought the girls might like some souvenirs. Something to take home for show and tell. Besides, she wanted to keep going. She felt as if she had to keep going. They piled into the car with Lenore and the girls in the back and Erroll began to drive. He drove more quickly this time along the coast road. He passed a truck carrying chickens, honking as he went. He had to pull quickly back into his lane. Marty glanced back at Lenore, shaking his head.

When Lenore looked up, she saw another car driving straight toward them. "Oh, my God!" she cried. "We're going to die." The girls screamed and Lenore pressed them down toward the floor. Marty, who sat in the front seat, braced his arms across the frame of the car as if he could hold it intact. There was no shoulder on the road, nothing they could do, except to drive straight toward the oncoming car, which at the last moment swerved back into its own lane and went rumbling past them down the road. Erroll shook his head as he drove on. "The duppy do that," he said.

Marty turned to Lenore. "Let's go back to the hotel."

"But there's nothing for us to do there," she said. Even the girls agreed, so Erroll turned off onto a road that headed up toward the mountains. As soon as he made his turn, the wind died down. Lenore wasn't sure when the paved road turned to dirt, but soon they were bracing themselves, bouncing over ruts. Now the road was lined with sheep and goats, toothless old women, some who reached out their hands, begging, and men in halter tops, sweaty, many carrying things on their heads.

The car swerved and twisted along the dusty road and birds suddenly appeared—colorful birds with red crests, blue-tipped wings. Without the wind and the sea air, the car turned very hot and Lenore felt a thin layer of dust settle on her skin. Whereas before they had winced at the wind, now they settled back into a kind of torpor. "Is it much further?" Marty asked after a time. Erroll shook his head. "Just a little ways now." But there was a mountain straight ahead, and no one lived on the mountain, so Lenore knew that they had to cross it.

The heat amazed her, the shock of it. She watched her girls wither and curl into fetal positions on either side of her, their long legs wrapped around one another in her lap. She sniffed their moist heads and smelled salt and sweat and sunscreen and another odor that was just their bodies, the bodies of little girls. Her arms hurt, but she didn't have the heart to move them. She tried to settle back, her arms falling asleep, the girls entwined across her as they had once been inside of her.

At last they stopped. Lenore must have drifted to sleep because when she looked up there were chickens, shacks with tin roofs, men with machetes chopping fruit. Erroll pulled over and said, "We can get out here. I'll get you something to drink."

Lenore roused the girls and pulled her arms free. Her arms lay numb at her sides and she got out of the car to shake them. She flapped them wildly and the girls began to laugh. Marty stood at the side of the road trying to take a picture of the men chopping fruit. Lenore was busy, shaking her arms, when suddenly she heard the men begin to shout. They picked up their machetes and started pounding them on the ground, on the melons they were carving, and beating them on the flat of their hands. Other men came out of their huts and they too started slapping their machetes on their hands and against their houses. They slapped and banged and soon the sound was deafening. Lenore looked around and saw Marty with the camera.

"Stop it, Marty," Lenore shrieked. "Put the camera down." She saw Erroll racing back across the dusty road, bottles of soda in his hand, shouting in a language she did not understand. Now the men were all shouting and Erroll was arguing with them, his hands covered with orange soda and

Coke that had spilled, but at least the pounding of the machetes had ceased.

"Give them money," Erroll told Marty. "Not a lot, but give them something." Then he turned to Lenore and said, "Camera worse than salt for keeping African people down."

They bought postcards in a small darkened hut and the girls bought rag dolls and straw hats; they bought baskets of straw spun into the shape of flowers.

Then Erroll invited them over to his house. "My wife has prepared something for you to eat." Marty was reluctant, but Lenore said they should go. Erroll led them up a dirt alleyway to a cinderblock house that sat in a dirt yard filled with scattered auto parts and a scrawny tree. Children, some dressed, some not, ran around with smudged faces, snotty noses. Inside the house a woman—a round, rather severe-looking woman—stood beside a table where she had prepared some bread and cheese, milk for the girls, and cold drinks. Marty gave Lenore a look that meant "Can we eat this stuff?" Lenore stared back at him. "You'd better," she mouthed.

"Oh, what nice little girls," the woman said. "I bet even you can't tell them apart. You know," she told Lenore, "I took care of the babies of a woman at the hotel once and she said, You take care of my babies so nice, I'm going to have you come and work for me."

"This is for you." Erroll interrupted his wife, handing Lenore a cup of hot broth.

"She said it so many times, but then she never wrote," his wife went on. "Who looks after your little girls?"

"They go to the school where I teach," Lenore said, staring into the drink Erroll had brought for her. She didn't want anything hot, but she didn't think she could refuse.

"It's the bark tea I made you for your neck," Erroll told her as he gave his wife a frown, after which she busied herself with some plates, putting cheese slices on them. "You didn't drink the other one, did you?"

"No, I guess I didn't," Lenore replied sheepishly. Now she drank the tea. It had a strange, bitter taste, like dirt, things taken from the ground. Her body turned warm inside and she felt herself grow dizzy, as if she were on a drug. The flies on the table seemed bigger than any flies she'd ever seen and the mud floor was filthier than she had imagined and Erroll's wife seemed to be laughing at her. They had a large bed tucked in one corner and small cots in other parts of the room. The big bed was unmade, the sheets tangled, and Lenore knew that when they lay down, they could not help themselves.

The sky was growing dark and Lenore was relieved when Erroll said they shouldn't stay long because he thought the storm was coming at last. They said good-bye and Erroll drove them down the road they had come from. All were relieved when they got back to the sea, though the girls complained that they wanted to go home. By *home* they meant Rockford, not the hotel. The sky turned darker so that it was almost night and the rain came. It came in sheets, driving coconuts and bananas from the trees. The waves churned up the sea grass that entrapped small yellow fish and dumped them on the shore as surely as if fishermen had caught them in their nets.

Erroll pulled over to the side of the road. "I can't see two feet in front of me," he said. There was a restaurant across the road and they made a run for it. They were soaked to the skin, laughing. The restaurant was a thatched hut and rain poured down on all sides. They sat in the center where water didn't drip and were waited on by the blackest men Lenore ever saw. They ordered red snapper with peas and rice (the only thing on the menu that night) and one of the men put on some music. Calypso.

A woman who was sitting at the bar got up and danced. She was a round woman, not heavy, but large, who wore a T-shirt too tight for her. When she moved, her whole body shook; the men paused. She rolled her hips in a circling motion. Then Erroll got up and he began to dance. Not with her, but next to her, his body swaying. He closed his eyes and moved to the beat.

Lenore stood up and tapped Marty on the shoulder. "Dance with me," Lenore said, her wet clothes clinging to her body.

Marty patted her on the rear with a laugh. "You've gotta be kidding."

"I'm serious." Lenore put her hands around his waist. "Dance with me." When he wouldn't get up, Lenore began to sway. She heard her girls groan and laugh, but she kept on swaying. She turned her hips, raising her arms above her head. In the distance she heard clapping, whistles, the voices of her daughters growing fainter. But mainly she heard the music. Her feet and her hands followed its beat. Even after it stopped, the music was still in her head.

That night Marty reached for her, but Lenore fell asleep so suddenly she would have no memory of drifting off. In the middle of the night, something woke her. She listened, but she heard no sound, except for the sounds of breathing. Heading to the window, she looked out and saw that the palm trees were still. She reached up to touch her neck and found that the pain was gone.

She opened the balcony doors and stood outside. The sky was clear and full of stars. And there against the full moon, rising into the sky, she saw people, dozens of people, hundreds of people, some very old with no teeth, and some just children. They moved slowly, a long procession of them. They did not fly like birds, flapping their wings. Rather they moved like swimmers, their arms pulling them through the ink-black sky.

In the morning Claire could speak and Crystie's hair had smoothed back down. They found their mother standing on the balcony, gazing at a restful sea where egrets waded by the shore. Embracing their mother they said, "Oh, Mommy, it's a beautiful day." The girls raced out in their pajamas, chasing the egrets that rose gracefully, moving away from the shore.

At breakfast they learned that all beach activities had resumed and the girls begged their parents to take them out again on the glass-bottom boat. Marty wouldn't go because he got seasick, but he helped them on board since Gosset refused to help. In fact, he seemed to act as if they weren't even there. As they sailed away, Marty gave them a little salute from the shore.

The boat moved smoothly across the surprisingly calm water. The girls squealed as they had before, pleading with their mother to look, but she refused. "I think I've seen enough," she said. Then she sat back, clasping the railing, and stared straight ahead.

About the Author

MARY MORRIS is the author of nine books: four novels, three collections of short stories, and two travel memoirs, including *Nothing to Declare: Memoirs of a Woman Traveling Alone.* Her most recent novel, *House Arrest,* was published in May 1996 by Nan A. Talese/Doubleday. She has also coedited with her husband, Larry O'Connor, *Maiden Voyages,* an anthology of the travel literature of women. Her numerous short stories and travel essays have appeared in such places as the *Paris Review,* the *New York Times,* and *Vogue.* The recipient of a Guggenheim Fellowship and the Rome Prize in Literature, Morris teaches writing at Sarah Lawrence College and lives in Brooklyn, New York, with her husband and daughter.